NOBLE V:
GREYLANCER
菊地秀行

NOBLE V: GREYLANCER

菊地秀行

HIDEYUKI KIKUCHI

TRANSLATED BY TAKAMI NIEDA

HAIKA SORU

SAN FRANCISCO

Noble V: Greylancer
Copyright © 2011 Hideyuki Kikuchi
Originally published in Japan by Asahi Shinbun Publications Inc.

English translation © 2013 VIZ Media, LLC
Design by Sam Elzway
All rights reserved.

Cover art © 2013 Vincent Chong

HAIKASORU
Published by VIZ Media, LLC
295 Bay Street
San Francisco, CA 94133

www.haikasoru.com

Library of Congress Cataloging-in-Publication Data

Kikuchi, Hideyuki, 1949–
  Noble V : Greylancer / Hideyuki Kikuchi ; Translated by Takami Nieda.
    pages cm
  ISBN 978-1-4215-5417-4
  1. Vampires--Fiction. I. Title.
  PL855.I3846N66 2013
  895.6'36--dc23
                                        2013008821

Printed in the U.S.A.
First printing, May 2013

DRAMATIS PERSONAE

GREYLANCER
Overseer of the Northern Frontier sector
The Nobility's greatest warrior

MAYERLING
Overseer of the Western Frontier sector

DUCHESS MIRCALLA
Overseer of the Southern Frontier sector

ZEUS MACULA
Overseer of the Eastern Frontier sector

VAROSSA
Longtime weaponsmith serving
House Greylancer

MICHIA
Villager from Ardoz who comes to the
wounded Greylancer's aid

LETICIA
Country girl from the Western Frontier who
happens upon the injured Greylancer

GALLAGHER
Marksman serving as Greylancer's retainer
after being captured

SHIZAM
Swordsman practicing the Streda style

CONTENTS

PROLOGUE:
A FRAGMENT FROM
A HISTORICAL TEXT

In the vermillion-colored tide of the Nobility's proud
history, no period illuminated their eminence more than the three
thousand years during which the Nobility contended against the
enormous boulder disrupting the raging current.

The Nobility magically manipulated science to their will and
confronted this enormous obstacle.

The enormous boulder was an enemy. An enemy from outer
space.

Even the Nobles, endowed with eternal life, might let slip a
mournful sigh at the mere thought of the endless depths of the
constellations. It was from there that the enemy known as the
Outer Space Beings—the OSB—came.

These three thousand years—tinted vermillion, stained crimson, marked by death shrouds and bloodshed—glorified the
Noble warriors. After enjoying five thousand years of peace,
with humanity held in servitude, for the first time, the Nobility
engaged in a daily battle that, aside from drinking the blood of
humans, might appropriately be called Evil's calling.

I shall spare you the particulars.

Only to say that the Nobility pitched themselves into battle
with a blood frenzy.

Black bats and pale-faced men tore across winter's moonlit
sky. Noble warriors stood against OSB aircraft. The enemy's
thunder tanks and single-seated tanks, their gold-chromed armor

protected by some invisible energy force, clashed against the Nobility's science and magic. In time, traveling troubadours sang their reverence, not for the grand battle, but for the vast wasteland turned burial ground.

The war took place in the Frontier, far from the Capital.

It was there the humans lived. The Frontier, a stark contrast to the splendor in which the Nobility lived, was where these trifling beings had been consigned—nay, allowed—to exist.

Ironically enough, it was because of humanity's very helplessness that the responsibility fell to the Nobles to protect the humans from the OSB invasion.

Many of the overlords—overseers of the Frontier—forfeited that responsibility, a fact that later became the root of humanity's distrust and the Nobility's eventual decline. Distrust joined with hate and turned into a rallying cry for revolt. Humanity left few records of the Nobility during this period. Hatred elected to extinguish rather than to chronicle.

However, humanity preserved the names of a select few in its annals.

Most of the names have already become legend and all but vanished, as if inscribed into crimson-colored history by a zephyr wind. The Nobles were remembered only in fragmentary verses of ballads and sagas. Yet some villagers in remote corners of the Frontier, defying the winds of time, strove to pass on the meaning of these names from generation to generation.

This is a story woven by their chapped lips and shuttered eyes, and also the first name to be spun out of blood, darkness, and moonlight.

CHAPTER 1:
GUARDIAN OF THE FRONTIER

1

At the onset of autumn in the year 7000 by Noble reckoning, two fears plagued the village of Ardoz.

One was the presence of the OSB—outer space beings that had been waging war against Ardoz's rulers, the Nobility, for over a hundred years. The other was the imminent visit from their overlord and overseer of the Northern Frontier sector, Greylancer.

Were this a different sector or an inspection by a local overseer, the villagers would not have much cause to fret. An overseer's appearance in a human habitat zone was exactly that—a ceremonious procession of auto-vassals flanking a G-coffin paraded down the street, all accompanied by the solemn music of a robotic band. Nary a soul believed that an inspector, much less a lord, was acting as the menacing eye of the Nobility from inside the coffin as decreed in the missive from the Capital.

But the overlord of the Northern Frontier sector would surely come.

For over three thousand years, the Greater Noble Greylancer had ruled over this sector, becoming a legend in his lifetime. His very appearance inspired awe in his subjects.

But the villagers were shaken by a peculiar kind of confusion and anxiety.

As the appointed time approached, they glanced up at the source of their confusion, the sky itself. White clouds frolicked in the blue sky like kittens. Not even a shadow of OSB aircraft, rumored to have come from the endless void to engage the Nobility night and day in a fierce aerial battle, passed overhead.

No, it was daylight.

Lord Greylancer was expected to arrive at high noon.

In two minutes' time. But just how was a Noble—a vampire—capable of visiting this sun-drenched village?

"Are you sure this isn't some sham, Chief?" the sub-chief, one of ten villagers standing at the north entrance, asked Chief Lanzi. "I know he's a Greater Noble and all, but in the middle of the day? How do you reckon he'll get here? And bringing with him only one retainer?"

"I won't pretend to understand the ways of the Nobility—of all the villages in the Frontier, coming to a speck of dust such as this. I suppose you and I will go to our graves never knowing."

"But I heard he'd been here once before, when you were a boy."

The wrinkled chief pried open his fissured eyes and blinked. "You heard right. I was four. My mother and father forbade me, but I cracked open the window and snuck a peek at the path in front of my house. I heard the sound of hooves clopping from a distance, and soon enough, this towering shadow straddling a gargantuan horse passed before my eyes. It felt as if a ghostly presence blew in through the window. I couldn't sleep a lick that night. That was the Noble Greylancer."

"But that was at night, wasn't it?"

"Yeah, a brilliant moon shone down over the village."

"He aims to come in broad daylight this time. Did vampires evolve somehow when we weren't looking?"

"Who knows what the Nobility are up to? At least he doesn't need any more than three delegates to greet his arrival. The rumor is that the Southern and Eastern overlords demand a welcome parade costing villages a year's revenue."

"Nothing for you to be happy about." The sub-chief bit a bent finger. "All I've heard is how cruel and cold-blooded his lordship is, like a messenger from hell. And he's coming to this tiny village in the shining sun. I tell you, Chief, this is an omen. A sign of bad things to come. Something beyond our imagination."

"Shh!" The village treasurer tensed, his eyes fixed on a point in the distance. "I hear hooves…he's coming!"

The lingering villagers disappeared at once, as if scattered by an ominous black wind.

Only four remained.

The chief, sub-chief, treasurer, and…a redheaded woman. Though a hard life had aged her, she was still in her early thirties. She was the chief's wife.

It was obvious by the way her husband eyed her like a nuisance that her presence was unwelcome.

After arguing with her husband much of the morning, she had joined the welcome delegation against his wishes.

And when two shadows on horseback appeared in the path stretching down the miasma-draped wasteland, the look on the woman's face resembled one of enchantment, unlike the terror-stricken faces of the men next to her.

One by one, the faces vanished from windows and doors of mud-packed houses made of wood and stone. The threadbare curtains were drawn.

Though appearing to be shrouded by a dark mist from afar, the figure halting the black cybernetic horse before them was blurred by a navy and gold-tinged haze. Navy was the color of his cape, gold the color of the embroidery on his coat.

"We've been expecting you. I am Lanzi, Chief of Ardoz village. This is Sub-Chief Sdao, and the village treasurer, Shijog."

"Pardon the trouble. I am Greylancer." The voice from atop the horse sounded terribly distant, but packed enough force to send chills up the spines of the four villagers.

Long shiny black hair, a rugged face as if the bones underneath were forged from steel, a neck thick enough to support that weight, thick brows, tall nose, his tightly drawn lips red like blood. One bellow from those lips might fell birds in flight. As well, his body appeared as if flesh and skin were stretched over a steel frame. His eyes were as blue and deep as the ocean but would no doubt turn as red as his lips at the first whiff of blood.

Greylancer jerked his chin toward the mounted figure behind him and said, "My retainer, Grosbec."

The man, bowing with his hands still gripping the reins, was narrow-chested and neither as tall nor broad around the shoulders as his master. Chief Lanzi imagined his delicate head popping off with a flick of his master's finger and blowing away into the horizon with a single breath. The mechanized armor beneath his cape appeared utterly useless or rather, in eternal disrepair.

Thin, slight brows, half-lidded eyes that appeared shut, eyes like those of dead fish, and finally a look of agony as if he'd taken his last gasp. Despite the sword hanging at his side and the laser gun affixed to his right forearm, he hardly seemed able to handle them. No doubt they were broken anyway.

Nevertheless, the expression that Greylancer directed at his only companion was one of complete trust. "Anything?" Greylancer asked Grosbec.

The villagers stared at one another in confusion.

"No different than the other villages. Inevitable, I'm afraid." Grosbec rubbed the base of his nose, in the manner of the drug addicts in the village.

"Anyone?"

"I cannot say for certain. No one within earshot."

"Good," said the voice of steel. "Whatever they might feel for the Nobility cannot be helped."

"Yes, my lord." The man with the voice and body of an invalid pinched his nose harder.

When Greylancer dismounted his horse, the villagers heard the earth rumble—a phantom sound, of course. But no wonder—the Noble stood nearly two meters tall.

Greylancer's deep blue eyes paused on the woman and reflected her smile before turning to the chief. "Do you find it strange to see us walking in the sun?" he asked.

"Why, er…no."

"You needn't hide your shock. At present, only Grosbec here and I are capable of doing so."

"My lord," said the chief, dropping his eyes in deference.

Greylancer's gaze reverted to the woman. "A rare surprise seeing a woman to greet our arrival."

"Begging your pardon," said the chief. "This is my wife."

"My name is Michia." The woman bowed, perhaps to conceal the forlorn look on her face.

"Do vampires not frighten you?"

"Why, not in the least."

"Well now…" Greylancer smiled faintly. Awl-like incisors peered out from lips that were blanched for a vampire. "Quite a woman. But rest assured. We'll not stay long. We have been traveling the sector, but this village was not one of our planned stops. We've come because a surveillance satellite reported something falling from the sky in this area."

Though the villagers had heard of the existence of several dozen surveillance satellites floating on the outer edges of the atmosphere, they were ignorant of the particulars of their use. Nevertheless, it was enough to fill the village chief and the others with apprehension. *Something falling from the sky…* The overlord had ridden his horse to investigate this *something* himself, in all likelihood, to dispose of it.

Chief Lanzi swallowed hard.

Greylancer towered over him like a giant. Unarmed. He carried neither lance, nor bow, nor sword. No one doubted his ability to crush any enemy regardless.

"Are you speaking of the OSB?" the chief asked, fearing he would incur the overlord's wrath for speaking out of turn.

But Greylancer smiled faintly a second time. "Indeed," he answered. "You know well. A worthy subject. Any ideas?"

2

Chief Lanzi turned to the others. The sub-chief and treasurer shook their heads.

"Wait…" It was Michia whose face clouded. As the men's gazes converged on her, she continued, "I saw the woodcutter Beijrot this morning, when I went foraging for mushrooms in the northern forest. He said something about watching a shooting star drop into the forest last night."

"When was that?"

"I…didn't ask."

"Hmm, do you know the approximate location?"

Michia's eyes narrowed and her brows knitted as she searched her memory. Two seconds later, her eyes opened wide. "The northern forest is about twenty kilometers from this village. And then another fifty kilometers from Beijrot's cabin to the deep forest."

The Noble shot a look northward. "Is this woodcutter home now?"

"Yes," answered the treasurer. "Someone saw him leaving the village not three hours ago."

"Any inhabitants near the impact point?"

"Yes, the homes of four woodcutters," Chief Lanzi answered.

"Their numbers?"

"One family is expecting a child any day now, but including the child, seventeen."

Greylancer nodded. "We will take our leave. You are all to stay inside your homes. And—" He uttered something peculiar. "If the woodcutter and his family return, do not let them into your homes. Should they attempt to enter, kill them."

An air of unease besieged the four villagers. The Noble's every utterance affected the fates of humans living in the Frontier. Would this fistful of powder pitched into the flames cause an innocuous gunshot or a blasting charge?

"What ever do you mean?"

Greylancer regarded the chief's terrified visage and answered in a low bass, "Do not fret. Do as I say, and you will be safe. Understand? Assuming familiarity with anyone will instantly lead to your demise. Let us meet again." Then he muttered, "Let's go" to Grosbec, and with a dark blue boot, kicked the cybernetic horse into a full gallop, whipping up a whirlwind around them.

Watching the riders receding between the houses, Chief Lanzi remarked, "What skill handling the reins and the horse. At their rate, it won't take but a half hour to reach the northern end," after which he turned to his wife and said, "From the way you were acting, I suspected you knew him, but perhaps I was wrong. His lordship didn't even bat an eye. What a relief."

"Come now," Michia said, flashing a disbelieving smile. But when the men began to return to their homes, she looked back in the direction where not even a shadow of the vampire remained. She stared down at the point where he had stood. It was obvious that the thoughts swirling in her mind differed completely from those of the others.

†

The ride to Beijrot's cabin did not take ten minutes.

Both Greylancer's and Grosbec's cybernetic horses had been custom built.

A tiny cabin slumbered beneath the shadow of a branch of a liza tree standing a hundred meters tall.

Greylancer went inside the cabin and immediately came out. "No one inside. From the look of the ashes in the fireplace, he must have gone out again as soon as he returned from the village. No horse. Anything?"

The mounted Grosbec had taken on a different complexion. The color had returned, the unhealthy stiffness was gone from not only his face but also his entire body, and a faint smile flickered across his lips. "At present, I sense only animals within two kilometers," was the answer to his master's query.

"We should have asked if the woodcutter is the curious type."

"Indeed."

"He seems to have a dog, but there is no sign of him. Let us go."

They rode another ten kilometers, whereupon a cabin larger than Beijrot's peered out from behind a grove of trees on the right.

"Anything?"

"No."

They repeated the short exchange another three times, once for each time they passed a woodcutter's house that Michia had spoken of.

When they came within a few kilometers of the edge of the forest, Greylancer pulled up on the reins.

Clear of trees now, approximately two hundred meters ahead in the ochre-colored mesa, there lay what appeared to be a blue metallic object that was clearly not of this world. Its brilliant sheen accentuated the desolation of the treeless wilderness surrounding it.

It resembled a saucer with three horizontal tail planes. A two-seater judging by its ten-by-eight-meter size. The two open bulges on what appeared to be the cockpit corroborated this. The body was split open diagonally from the rear of the cockpit to the tail, such that it was difficult to believe the aircraft had crash-landed safely.

The landing had not put a mark on it. The enemy aircraft was not equipped with an energy shield but was made of a super-dense alloy.

A human shadow stood in front of the cockpit.

Spiked leather vest and wool shirt. The wide-barrel hunting pistol was nicked and well worn, but the hand axe stuck behind his belt was shiny enough to reflect one's face.

Another larger axe lay at his feet. No doubt this was the woodcutter.

Rather than the tool of his chosen profession, he held a cylindrical tube with a grip resembling that of a handgun.

He stood at a distance of five meters and pointed the cylinder at the aircraft.

A pale blue mass spewed forth from the tube, and in a moment the aircraft, taking on the same hue, became enveloped in a brilliant glow. When the glow subsided, not a trace of the aircraft remained. Scattered about the sandy earth and rocks were silver dust particles, which blew away in a blast of wind.

The woodcutter fell to his knees, clasped his hands in front of his chest, and began to drone some kind of incantation.

"That was a first," said Greylancer, narrowing his eyes.

"I hear the OSB have no blood running through their veins." Grosbec tightened his grip on the reins.

"Stay here." Greylancer spurred his horse forward.

Even as he drew within ten meters of the supplicant figure, the woodcutter was still, seeming not to notice the Noble's presence.

Climbing off his horse, Greylancer called out, "Beijrot?"

So engrossed was the woodcutter in prayer that he spun around in shock. He stared at the giant with the deep blue cape fluttering in the wind. "Who—are you?" he asked, distorting his bearded face.

"Are you Beijrot?"

"Yeah. But...you wouldn't be..."

"Greylancer."

"Oh, your lordship! Yes, I am Beijrot. What are you doing here in these parts?"

"I came with questions, but they have been answered. This dust scattered about you—the remains of the woodcutters and their families, Beijrot?"

"What...was that?" The woodcutter staggered backward. "I came out to investigate the thing that fell out of the sky last night, is all."

"If you merely came to investigate, why did you disintegrate the aircraft? Which weapon will that arm behind your back reach for? The axe of the woodcutter whose identity you've stolen or your blaster? Which would be easier to handle in your present form?" Beijrot continued to inch backward. The sweaty, quaking figure was outwardly one of a simple, mild-mannered woodcutter. "Or perhaps neither. You must know your weapons are ineffective against vampires." Greylancer brought his left hand up to his ear. The jewel on his ring finger reflected the sun's rays. "Well now, this is what my retainer tells me you were thinking just now: *Damn Nobles! Someday, we'll wipe out the lot of you!*"

"Right you are!" Beijrot jumped right and pointed the cylinder at Greylancer. A glowing blue mass again fired from the tube, and the vampire vanished into thin air. "Yes!" Beijrot howled and wiped the sweat off his brow with his weapon hand. The awful tension drained from him, like paint dissolving in water. "Who said the beings on this planet were immortal? I got him! The son of a bitch is nothing but a speck of dust now!"

Suddenly, the triumphant voice turned to shrieks of pain.

Beijrot grabbed at the silver head of the lance sticking easily a meter out of his solar plexus, but not before he found himself lifted three meters off the ground.

Laughing cruelly as the helpless woodcutter twitched in convulsions was none other than Greylancer.

Had not a blast lethal enough to destroy an atomic nucleus just incinerated him? And where had he been concealing a three-meter lance?

"Answer me one question and I shall put you out of your misery in one blow, you filthy outer-space invader. Where is the other varmint?"

Greylancer gave the lance a cruel shake.

Fresh blood spurted out of Beijrot's mouth. His shrieks turned into screams.

"Still able to keep this form, are you? Never you mind. You shall suffer a painful death. Pray to your god."

Greylancer brought down his lance with one swing, splitting the woodcutter's body down the middle.

Fresh blood pelted the ground first and then the human entrails splattered down atop it.

The transformation occurred a few seconds later.

Split asunder by one fell swing, the two halves began to melt in the sun. The eyeballs, flesh, and bone revealed themselves as shams as they all liquefied into gray mucus and oozed in Greylancer's direction. It managed to creep about a meter before halting its advance over the yellow earth.

After waiting several seconds to confirm the OSB's death, Greylancer shook the lance one last time. Every last drop of the gray blood spattered the ground. He lowered his lance and called Grosbec's name.

3

A voice inside Greylancer's head answered:

I'll be there in a moment.

Soon, Grosbec appeared out of the trees on horseback and pointed the horse toward his master.

When his servant was but ten meters away, Greylancer spied a black shadow dropping down from overhead.

"Take cover!" Greylancer yelled, too late—

A bloody mass shot out of Grosbec's heart, and Grosbec toppled forward off his horse.

A steel arrow. Greylancer glanced down at the arrowhead buried deep in the ground and swung his lance.

There was a beautiful clang of metal as a second and third arrow fell out of the sky.

So he was no ordinary woodcutter, thought Greylancer, and then a bloodied voice crept inside his mind.

My lord, the enemy is a ghost archer.

Grosbec's thoughts. Greylancer slapped the rear of his cybernetic horse, sending the steed cantering away, and darted toward his loyal companion lying on the ground.

He also sent Grosbec's mount away and struck down a fourth arrow.

Grosbec's body was already beginning to disintegrate. His
pale skin was sallow and emitting a haze of decay.

*He must have been in one of the four houses, disguised as a visitor.
I will avenge you in a moment.*

To a dying man, perhaps his tone sounded heartless.

The Greater Noble stood up. He hoisted his lance above his
head and threw it without taking aim.

The lance vanished, leaving behind a loud buzz. Only the
two vampires present understood that it was flying toward the
OSB that had loosed the arrow that had pierced Grosbec's heart.

My lord?

Grosbec's shock ran through his master's mind. A black arrow
sprouted from the right side of Greylancer's chest. It had struck
him when he threw the lance.

It's all right. It missed my heart.

Greylancer wrapped his left hand around the shaft and plucked
out the arrow with neither wince nor shudder.

*Hurry…you must return…to the village. Iron-tipped arrow…
look after the wound…or your insides…will decay.*

Will you survive?

That was a question to which Greylancer already knew the
answer. Among those serving him, the men with telepathic abilities
numbered fewer than five. Grosbec was among the precious few.

Even a telepath with the ability to read and transmit thoughts
within a kilometer radius was defenseless against an attack outside of his "earshot." Greylancer took to one knee next to his
irreplaceable servant.

I believe not.

Grosbec's thoughts sounded oddly clear and lucid in the
Noble's mind.

Where will you go?

*Perhaps the Sacred Ancestor was right, my lord. Now that my
end is near, I finally understand his words.*

Transient guests are we.

Indeed. Even as we've attained immortality, I leave you now. I pray you will never come to feel the same way that I do.

With a start, Greylancer looked up and stared off into the distance.

"Between the eyes," he said aloud. The Noble was capable of sensing the outcome of his lance attack from two thousand meters away.

There, I have avenged your fall. Go now, rest in peace. You need not worry about your wife and boy.

I am grateful...how strangely peaceful...

Greylancer paused for a moment and then stood up.

There were piles of grayish-blue dust packed around Grosbec's cape and armor. One pile, which poured out from the right sleeve, held the shape of an open hand until the wind blew it away.

Taking a deep breath, Greylancer gathered up Grosbec's garments and murmured, "OSB—you will pay dearly for his life."

†

At the outset of war a hundred years prior, both the Nobility and OSB were shocked to discover the powers they had in common.

Whereas the Nobility turned other creatures into one of their own and controlled their wills by feeding upon their blood, the OSB wielded the same influence over humans via the power of metamorphosis. But though they were able to assume the form of others, the OSB were incapable of breeding like the Nobility.

The Nobility stood at a tremendous advantage in the beginning. The OSB's primary weapon was an atomic blaster capable of incinerating objects, but the Nobility were able to reconstitute their forms after being struck by the sizzle of plasma.

The OSB were thrown into perfect confusion. The way the immortal Nobility were able to rise again from an atomic blast was beyond comprehension—beyond even their concept of regeneration.

Regeneration, as the OSB understood it, signified cell reproduction at the atomic level. Vampire resurrection defied analysis.

That the Noble garments, too, rematerialized intact shocked and terrified the OSB. They repeated meticulous tests on capes and rings and various other spoils, only to find that they were made of ordinary silk and cotton. Though the pieces had been specially engineered to restore their shape after experiencing primitive sword and gun damage, they could easily be burned to cinders. Nevertheless, these same items were reconstituted from ash along with their wearers.

It was not until a year later, when—as gleaned from human knowledge—they drove a stake into a Noble's heart, that the OSB grew wiser to the supernatural forces fueling vampiric existence. Only when they bore witness to the Noble succumbing to death's call, his flesh along with his garments crumbling to dust, did the OSB finally understand the words—*legend, curse, occult,* and *evil*—swirling inside the memories of their human prey.

Though the Nobles were vulnerable to natural sunlight, they were impervious to the artificial light produced by the OSB. Wooden stakes were ineffective unless driven precisely into their hearts. Even if his head were severed at the neck, a vampire could come back from the dead, its head reattached in a matter of seconds. But only if reattached within ten minutes.

Such phenomena were best understood as supernatural rather than physical, but since the OSB were only capable of processing reality within the material realm, these supernatural beings shook the OSB and wreaked havoc with their primitive DNA memory.

Had the OSB not learned, from consuming human knowledge, that a wooden stake or steel blade to the heart would destroy their enemies, the war would have lasted less than a month, much less the century of attrition the human pawns had endured.

The knowledge of their human victims aided the OSB. Enlightened now by humanity's age-old slaying methods, the OSB took human shape, infiltrated the realms of their immortal enemies, and drove stakes through their hearts. They destroyed the Nobility's defense shields, and the OSB's mother ship launched warships and aircraft to rain countless steel blades down upon the Nobility during the day while they slept. The blades pierced through Noble coffins, skewering the sleeping vampires in the heart.

The Nobility mounted a counterstrategy with dimensional shields and telepaths.

They recruited humans and Nobles that possessed extrasensory powers and dispatched them throughout the land, save for the Capital where few humans dared live.

Before the OSBs in human form could brandish their stakes, the telepaths, sensing their murderous intent, aided the Nobility in felling the intruders.

Until the covert presence of these telepaths had come to light, the OSB invasion had stalled.

Shifting their target from the Nobility to the telepaths, the OSB now waged an offensive against these formidable psychic counterspies.

As rare as the telepaths were to begin with, their decimation threatened the very survival of the Nobility. The vampires protected and harbored them, and after DNA analysis of the surviving psychics, the Nobility endeavored to engineer new telepaths by breeding the best of their kind.

The past century of war had seen the rise and fall of generations of telepaths, with Greylancer just now losing one of a precious few.

†

Greylancer returned to the village of Ardoz an hour later.

The blue winter sky began to grow dark.

Chief Lanzi greeted Greylancer in the public square, which looked as if it might be crushed by the cold and coming darkness. "Your lordship."

Noting Grosbec's conspicuous absence, the chief bowed with a smile belying his sadness. The villagers milling about the square had retreated to their homes when the watchtower alerted them to Greylancer's arrival.

"How many have come to the village during my absence?"

"Four, your lordship," answered Chief Lanzi. "One was a traveling medicine man, another a sword grinder, the third was a villager returning from an errand in a neighboring village, and lastly a traveler en route to Jarmusch."

"Any of the travelers still here?"

"No, they stopped in for a drink at the tavern and went on their way. The watchtower guards can confirm their departure."

"What of those tending to their crops?"

"Yes, I have word that they've all returned not too long ago."

Frontier towns like Ardoz counted the numbers coming and going from the village in order to prevent raids by bandits—and now to keep out the dreaded usurpers, the OSB.

"I will take lodging at your abode tonight. We have matters to discuss."

The color drained from the chief's face. "Uh…shall I arrange for anyone to join us?"

"*After* we've talked."

The giant dismounted from his horse, and his dark blue cape fluttered majestically.

†

Michia came out of the house upon Lanzi and Greylancer's arrival.

The couple's son was not at home, and Lanzi's daughter had been adopted when Michia came to live with the chief. Now the girl lived with a farming family in the Northern Frontier.

After sending Michia away, Chief Lanzi was confronted by the sheer fact that a Noble stood in his parlor. The sight of the vampire lowering his frame onto the sofa was enough to stifle his breathing. The last glimmer of daylight streamed in through the window, spreading the Noble's shadow over the room as if to shroud it in darkness.

Then, Greylancer revealed a scenario that made the chief's blood curdle.

"I'd assumed there were only two, but when I checked the OSB's weapon, it had discharged one blast fewer than the number of woodcutters' family members. One of them must have survived."

"But…none of the other woodcutters have been to the village today."

"You said that the villagers went out to tend their crops."

Just as Chief Lanzi began to nod, his face went blank—the meaning of Greylancer's remark registered in his mind. "Are you suggesting one of the OSB first took the identity of a woodcutter and then switched to the form of one of the villagers?"

"I don't know. It is possible. If there is the slightest possibility, it bears investigating."

"How do you propose to do that?"

"You will alert the village that I will be patrolling the premises. That's all. The villagers will wait for dawn sheltered in their homes—all except one."

"You mean to expose yourself to draw out the enemy?"

"A tired ploy, I realize. But that it has not fallen out of favor is proof of its efficacy."

"As you wish." Wiping the sweat from his face, the chief contemplated the human-shaped specter before him. Just whose defeat was best for the village, he knew not.

CHAPTER 2:
EXTERMINATING
THE INTRUDERS

1

The third OSB had stolen the form of one of the woodcutter's family members, headed straight for Ardoz, and, after transforming into one of the villagers toiling in the fields, returned to the village. Since it retained the knowledge and outward appearance of its victim, not even family members could see through its trickery.

Perhaps Ardoz was not the OSB's destination or hiding place at all. The Glacierites lived in a town not fifty kilometers away, where it was possible to board a ship and sail down the River Benev.

Greylancer had decided to return because Michia had told Beijrot of Greylancer's visit before the woodcutter's body had been stolen by the OSB.

If the OSB could steal the identity of the Greater Noble, whose name was known across the Frontier, they would be able to march into the Capital uncontested. No doubt the enemy would risk life and limb to that end.

As darkness descended, Greylancer left the chief's house.

The eyes of those peering from the windows converged on the Noble patrolling the streets.

He emerged into the village square.

Though the streetlamps were dark, a near-full moon lit the well and stone relief with a bluish glow. Several wagons were parked on the western edge.

Greylancer looked up in the direction of the grating screech overhead.

Silhouetted birds fluttered across the moon. Night migrants. The black nocturnal birds of passage alighted around Greylancer and began pecking at the shadows of the trees, houses, and wagons.

The birds used their pointed beaks to eat the ground insects gathered in the shadows at night, and because they appeared to be pecking at the shadows, they were also called "shadow eaters."

After gazing down for a moment at the birds picking the strandlike insects off the ground, Greylancer muttered, "Seems I lack what the shadow eaters are looking for." Nobles cast no shadows at their feet. "The night is still young. I pray the OSB are an impulsive race. The loss of Grosbec will be felt dearly," he grumbled to himself. Spoken by this man, however, the words had the ring of scathing damnation against the OSB. "A fine moon." After looking up for a moment, the Noble resumed his patrol.

He made no sound when he walked. Even the shadow eaters did not notice his footfall.

Of the paths leading out of the square, Greylancer headed for the west exit.

As he passed by the wagons parked at the edge, the nearmost wagon instantly began to lose its shape.

An amorphous mass the color of the wagon leapt at Greylancer.

The flash of movement gave away its presence. Greylancer twisted his enormous body to the right at an unthinkable speed.

Gripped in his right hand was the long lance he'd used to fell the ghost archer earlier in the day. The curved conical tip struck the mass and flung it against the stone wall along the path. The enemy was protean, shifting form moment by moment.

The instant the lance poised for another attack, the mass twisted into a vortex and flowed through a hole in the stone wall.

"Tch!" The Noble thrust the lance against the wall.

The wall exploded and smashed to pieces. When he cleared the rubble in his path, he spotted the fleeing mass fifty meters ahead.

NOBLE V: GREYLANCER   35

Suddenly, the mass changed shape again, stealing the form of a nearby creature. A black cat scampered fifty meters in the moonlight toward a lit building with unbelievable agility. The OSB was capable of doubling the abilities of the creatures it became.

Greylancer's lance discharged a particle beam. A purple streak tore through the darkness. The beam grazed the cat's tail and bore a five-meter-long trench in the ground. The explosion made no sound, as if in deference to the tranquility the moon demanded.

Watching the cat disappear inside the building, Greylancer broke into a run.

When he reached the door, lively music filled his ears. He didn't need to look at the sign to know he had stumbled into the all-night tavern found in every Frontier town.

The tavern was crowded with patrons.

The moment they glimpsed the stranger's entrance, the faces of the patrons and bartender-cum-proprietor froze. The room reeked of smoke and liquor.

"Not one move," commanded Greylancer before anyone could speak. "Anyone else here?" he asked, glancing at one door in the back and another to the left. The back door was the entrance into the staff room, and the door on the left led into the washroom.

Game maps for a vampire hunting game that was all the rage in the Frontier and coins and various chips and cards for wagering cluttered the tabletops. No one attempted to hide the game, perhaps petrified by the Greater Noble's ghostly aura.

"Two," the bartender-cum-proprietor answered, his voice stiff, perhaps surpassing the usual tremulous reaction. "My wife is in the back changing. And there is another in the toilet."

"Look right," boomed Greylancer to the patrons of the tavern. "If the person next to you has never left your sight, stand over there against the right window. Otherwise, raise your right hand."

Within seconds, everyone save the proprietor stood by the window. Despite the knives and guns undoubtedly concealed among them, not one thought to reach for their weapons, as they all stared at the same two doors Greylancer did.

The enemy could not have escaped. It must have taken some damage by the earlier hit. Neither was the enemy so feeble as to flee in the face of a flesh-and-blood Noble.

Since the enemy might be among the patrons, Greylancer had no choice but to detain them.

The back door opened first.

A slender middle-aged woman, wearing a colorful corset and flared skirt, emerged from the staff room and became immediately petrified by the tension in the room.

"A N-Noble…!" she stammered, and at the same, a youth in his mid-teens came out of the left door and was stopped cold.

"Lord Greylancer," the proprietor began to jabber. "This is my wife. And the boy there is my son. Whoever you're looking for, I can assure you these two aren't involved."

Whether the Greater Noble heard him or not, his steely voice rang across the tavern. "Strip off your clothes—both of you."

It was an order no one dared defy. Even the husband and father of the two in question could not form the words to protest.

Surely the two were desperate to know what they had done to attract such direct attention from a Noble. Surely they knew nothing. Nevertheless, the woman unlaced her corset, and the teen unbuttoned his shirt as ordered.

As the woman bared her ample breasts and taut body from the waist up beneath the gas lamp, the eyes of the patrons pleaded innocent to having any lascivious thoughts.

"Move your hands," ordered Greylancer. The woman lowered the hands covering her breasts. "Turn around."

Both mother and son turned once around.

Finally, anger began to seep into the eyes and faces of the patrons. They were not castrated livestock after all.

When Greylancer commanded, "Take off your bottoms," one of the men jumped up and shouted, "That's enough!" He pointed a gun at Greylancer.

The lance slashed the man's elbow like a bolt of lightning, sending the severed arm sailing toward the wall. So quick was

Greylancer's attack that the man was unaware of his pain until his blood rained down on the others like rose petals. He glanced around the blood-splattered room, then fell.

Strange occurrences happened all the time in the Frontier. But not even Greylancer could have predicted what happened next.

A gunshot rang out.

The gun, still gripped in the man's severed hand, had crashed against the wall and exploded on impact.

The bullet pierced the woman's right breast and shot clean through her back.

A dreadful silence came over the room, and in the next instant, the woman crumpled to the floor.

"Mama!" the boy shouted and ran to his mother.

Everyone stared in terror.

The woman's head twisted a full 360 degrees, tearing off at the neck, and sprang like a savage animal at Greylancer.

Deep inside the fanged mouth of the kindly countrywoman was the green glow of a cyclopean.

Greylancer thrust the lance inside her mouth, skewering the woman's head as it flew at him, then crushing it to pieces.

The room filled with screams.

Pulverized bits of flesh and bone and eyes turned into grayish ooze in midair and splattered on the poor onlookers' heads, faces, and hands.

Like the rest of the mother's body, the gray matter stuck on the people's skin twitched and quivered and stopped, until it vaporized in an instant.

"I shall take my leave of you." Greylancer spun on his heel, any interest in the tavern, its patrons, the OSB, the possessed woman, much less the village already leaving him.

Another gunshot.

A tiny hole opened in the cape shrouding his massive back and disappeared as quickly as it appeared. The Noble's garments were made of a memory fabric that restored its original shape when damaged.

Turning, Greylancer confronted the youth clutching the gun in both hands. Purple smoke plumed from the trembling barrel.

"You...killed my mother..." The boy sobbed. Tears rolled down his cheeks with every gasp.

The Noble's reply was frigid. "The creature that I struck down was not your mother. Don't you see that?"

"Listen to him, Lingor," shouted his father from behind the bar counter. "He's right!" He alone understood that the fate of his family turned on what would happen in the next few seconds. "Lord Greylancer is not responsible for what has happened here. Get ahold of yourself!"

"Nobles, Nobles, Nobles! They're to blame for all of this. Mama would still be alive if you damn Nobles—" The boy's anger tensed his finger before he'd intended to squeeze the trigger.

The moment the gun roared, Greylancer plunged the silver spearhead through the boy's throat, twisting the hilt for good measure. The boy's head tore off at the initial gouge and landed in the middle of where the patrons stood.

Screams again erupted from the crowd.

Lance in hand, Greylancer resumed his walk toward the door.

He sensed the hatred rise up and countless weapons being drawn behind him.

"Have you any idea the position you are in?" The force of his voice was enough to freeze the animosity surging toward him. "If the OSB are not destroyed within twenty-four hours of a confirmed infiltration, the area within a thousand kilometers of the invasion point will become the target of our corona cannon. I have yet to report to the Capital that the threat has been put down, and the woodcutter Beijrot made first contact with the OSB yesterday at dawn. Try as you might, there will be no escape."

Even after the echo of his voice and its master dissolved into the darkness, the villagers could not move for a good long while.

Several minutes passed, until freed from the curse at last, they began to tremble with newfound enmity and grief, while others counted the village's fortune at having been spared, thanks to the sacrifice of the tavernkeeper's family.

2

Greylancer left the tavern and headed directly for Chief Lanzi's house. His intention was to depart immediately.

He could give a damn about the collective hatred of the villagers. He had little interest in humanity to begin with. He was merely dispatching his duties as Frontier overlord. The truth was he could barely tolerate speaking to humans.

The overlordship was not determined by succession.

Before being appointed to this position by the Privy Council—the highest decision-making body of the Nobility—Greylancer had been a member of the Sub-Council and all but assured a seat in the next Privy Council.

The ladder up the ranks was a precarious one for which pedigree, skill, and proven record were requisite criteria. It was a great achievement for a Noble to earn a seat on the Sub-Council, much less the Privy Council. Yet Greylancer had easily ascended the elite ranks virtually uncontested.

The Noble Greylancer.

Though the Nobility had dispensed with such honorifics, his brethren naturally took to calling him by this appellation out of deference for his record for wiping out those among the Nobility opposed to the Sacred Ancestor.

In the Noble year 2004, the True Nobility World faction, which advocated the extermination of the human race, plotted to disperse a radioactive substance that selectively acted upon human DNA. It was the young warrior Greylancer that had killed every last one of the conspirators and foiled their plot on the eve of the operation.

And in the Noble year 3052, the Anti-Human Alliance, a larger, more powerful offshoot of the True Nobility World faction, set in motion a thousand-year conspiracy to assassinate the Sacred Ancestor. Two hundred years later, it was also Greylancer who exposed the plot within weeks and, risking his own ruin, drove a stake into the heart of the ringleader, a high-ranking member of the Privy Council.

And then again in the Noble year 3071, when humanity mounted an insurrection for the ages against the Nobility, leading the charge to put down the threat and punishing the regional Nobles that incited the uprising was none other than Greylancer.

Why this Greater Noble, embodying the full glory of the Noble race, was demoted to oversee a sector of the Frontier was a mystery even to the Privy Council handing down the order.

Nevertheless, Greylancer accepted the appointment without complaint and departed the Capital with his most trusted retainers in tow. Nearly ten thousand Nobles were said to have lined the street to soberly see off their exalted warrior.

Though he ruled over his subjects with both a gentle and severe hand, his disinterest in humans was not caused so much by this tavern incident alone as it was by Greylancer's nature.

Simply put, humanity's existence was beyond his comprehension. To most Nobles, humans were not much more than semiprecious vermin allowed to live only for the warm blood coursing through their veins.

When Nobles deigned to betray deep interest in humans, it was a matter of scholarship, and when the majority of Nobles gave any thought to humanity at all it was for the blood that could be got from their veins.

His business with this shit-smeared piddling town stinking of humans was done.

Upon reaching Chief Lanzi's house, Greylancer headed straight for the stable.

There he felt his knees go weak.

The reason was obvious. The effects of the ghost archer's arrow had drained his body. True to legend, though a wound from an iron arrow was not fatal, it was capable of burning and rotting the immortal flesh, causing infernal pain.

Such was the awesome will of the Greater Noble to endure for this long without batting an eye.

He was already inside the stable.

In a separate stall apart from Chief Lanzi's wagon and cybernetic horse were two tethered horses. One mount had only the burden of its master's garments.

Greylancer rose to his feet and staggered two steps in that direction before losing his balance again and toppling over.

The anger swelling on his face conveyed a shame for which not even death could atone.

Lurching like a boulder with arms and legs, Greylancer brought himself up on one knee.

And then he heard a gasp from outside the door.

The patter of footsteps, and then a pale hand rested on his shoulder.

"Were you watching, woman?" Neither an expression of gratitude nor joy, the Noble's words were imbued with a ghastly chill.

She seemed to tense for a moment and then quickly replied, "Yes, I was." The determination in her voice shook his look of menace. "Let me help you."

"Are you the chief's wife?"

"Michia, yes."

"Do not meddle where you do not belong."

"Yes, I know. But this an expression of my appreciation."

"Appreciation?" Greylancer's neck made a grinding sound as he twisted it in the woman's direction. "What are you talking about?"

"Come inside the house, if you care to know."

"No," he growled. "Move over there." His eyes gestured toward the pile of calorie weeds before him. The color and shape of an ordinary haystack, it was actually synthetic grass, the primary energy source for cybernetic horses.

Bearing down on one knee, he labored to his feet. The pit of his stomach burned like fire.

He shrugged off the woman's hand, sending her reeling several steps back, but she managed to keep her footing and returned to Greylancer's side, undeterred.

Again, her arm wrapped around his. No longer trying to break her hold, Greylancer lumbered forward and slumped against the pile of calorie weeds. Crushed under the weight of the giant, the haystack crackled like a mound of tiny crushed bones and compressed under him into a thick bed.

Michia repositioned him, threw open his cape, and found the wound on his stomach. A black stain seeped through his green and gold embroidered shirt and spread downward.

Michia nodded. "Stay here," she said and stood up.

"Wait. How did you know that I would return here? You were not outside."

"I've been waiting here in the stable. Knowing you, I expected you would come directly here without saying goodbye."

"*Knowing* me?"

"Yes, my lord." Nodding kindly, she twirled around and hastened out the door.

Within ten minutes, she returned with a white med case hanging from her shoulder.

Human medicine was useless in treating vampiric injuries. Michia hoisted the case, nonetheless, and revealed a false bottom. Greylancer's eyes glimmered at the sight of the items she produced from the case.

The red plastic packets were dehydrated blood. Were they discovered, the entire family would surely be crucified as servants of the Nobility. Even more astounding were the plastic vials stored in a cryogenic agent.

When Michia removed the lid from one of the vials pluming white smoke, a sweet bouquet crept into the Noble's nasal cavity.

"What is…?"

"My blood, your lordship. If we ever had occasion to meet, I wanted you to have a taste."

"You've been collecting blood?" Greylancer regarded the chief's winsome wife as if he were looking at an unfamiliar creature.

"Yes."

"It's true that human blood is the best elixir for healing my wounds. But if anyone should find this—"

"I would be torn to pieces, yes. No matter, I have cut my own wrists and collected the blood you see here, and another cache that I've collected over seventeen years is in a freezer in the basement."

"But why? What appreciation do you owe me?"

"In due time," Michia said. "Please drink first." Handing him the vial, she turned her back and waited.

"I am healed."

When Michia turned around, the vampire's mouth was painted crimson, a line of blood streaking from one edge of his lips and dripping off his chin.

She averted her eyes before Greylancer wiped the blood with the back of a hand.

"The blood is good. But I have no memory of the taste."

"If you did, I imagine I would be your servant instead of wedded to another."

"I don't understand."

"Seventeen years ago—perhaps the years mean nothing to you—I was fifteen years old. One summer day, my school had planned a field trip by steam bus." Michia took the unfinished vials from Greylancer's hand and returned them to the case. Her distant look seemed to reflect the sweetness of the memory.

Buoyed by good weather and the steady performance of the bus, the class ventured twice as far as they'd planned to go to the western forest.

She began picking flowers and gathering various edible plants, and by the time she looked up, darkness had already unfurled in the western sky.

The teacher chaperone turned pale. After boarding the students onto the bus and departing back to the village, he realized he'd left one girl behind.

"That girl was me. When I realized that I'd strayed from the group, I found myself in an old, magnificent abandoned graveyard. A thoroughly devastated ruin. Gravestones were overturned; the names engraved on them were scraped off and unreadable. The earth had been torched with gasoline. It must have been a Nobility graveyard destroyed back in the days of the human uprisings. Only the doors of the tomb were untouched by the devastation. A most ominous and beautiful graveyard. I understand now the entire property had been proportionately designed to appear aesthetically pleasing, but at the time, I simply could not tear myself away from the wicked beauty of the place."

And then she came to another realization—her classmates were long gone and she was utterly surrounded by darkness.

Terror embraced her entire being. When she started running in the direction of the bus, Michia heard the sound of stone grinding against stone behind her. She did not need to turn around to recognize that the tomb door had opened. Or that something had risen from the tomb and was now lurking behind her.

The putrid odor of soil assaulted her nostrils, penetrating her consciousness until she grew light-headed. She collapsed into his cold embrace.

A voice whispered in her, "So very warm. And delicious."

3

"You've cut your finger. Was it a blade of grass, perhaps? You have shaken me out of my slumber. My body swells for this tiny life. Allow me to sample a taste."

The smell of decay and dirt drew closer to Michia's neck.

It was at that moment another voice called out, "Wait."

"That voice reverberated frostily but forcefully in my mind. In that instant, I was able to escape the curse of the dark presence behind me.

"'She is a subject of my sector, Lord Joyceron,' said the voice.

'I am Greylancer, your successor as overlord of this sector.'

"It was the first time your name was burned into my heart.

"'I know you, Greylancer,' the voice behind me said. 'I have felt the passing of time from inside my grave. I have known about you since your youth. Do not interfere.'

"'You were relieved of your post as overlord for fomenting the human uprisings. If you lay a finger on one of my subjects, I will have to intervene.'

"'You dare oppose another Noble to protect a human?'

"'That, too, is the Nobility's fate.'

"The shadow behind me leapt at my rescuer, tracing an arc over my head. Then there was a strange sound as I glimpsed the spearhead pierce its black-caped back. In an instant, the shadow fell to the ground, dust."

In the darkness, Michia had recognized an even darker shadow with a great lance in its outstretched hand. The sinister figure stood against the night as if it might penetrate the darkness.

Michia stood motionless, unable to speak.

The figure that had rescued her from one horror was a horror himself. But the emotion swelling inside her heart was neither terror nor fear, but excitement.

Greylancer, she recognized, was none other than the name of the current overlord.

Those around Michia condemned the Noble as the devil, citing legends of countless atrocities he'd perpetrated. Michia believed in those legends.

Yet how strong, rugged, fierce, and gentle was this immoveable mountain of a man before her.

Saved from the clutches of a cursed death. Perhaps given the extreme prejudice she'd previously had, her impression of the Noble had been completely overturned.

Much to her shock, Michia had found herself in love with Greylancer from that moment.

"Are you all right?" the shadow asked, a voice like steel.

"Yes," answered Michia, in a voice that was unexpectedly clear.

"Good. Then go."

"It seems I've been left behind. I am alone here." Then she uttered a question that even she could hardly believe. "Would you take me back to Ardoz?"

"Do you know who I am?"

"Yes, you are Lord Greylancer, overseer of the Northern Frontier."

"And you ask me to return you to your village?"

"Why yes. You said that it is your duty to protect us, just before."

The shadow fell silent. Michia sensed something tremendous and inexpressible roiling inside the giant.

It soon subsided and hardened into steel.

"Very well. But swear this. You will never speak of your time with me."

"I swear," Michia answered immediately and then added, "Why?"

"Do not ask." His earth-rattling voice shook Michia's heart.

"I understand."

At last, the girl realized that her rescuer was unmistakably a Noble.

And now she spoke before him again, in the stables of her husband. "You departed first and I followed you out of the forest. In the moonlight, I could make out a single-passenger wagon—no, a chariot made of gold and steel—which you helped me onto. You then escorted me back to my village. Rocking in that chariot by your side was a most heartwarming time. The cries of the night birds or cursing winds did not frighten me. I yearned to ride to the ends of the earth with you. After you dropped me at the edge of town, I watched you ride off and I wept. I have been dead ever since."

Michia finished recounting her childhood incident quietly and with great feeling.

Greylancer's reaction was immediate. "I do not recall," said the voice of steel.

Michia could find not a foothold from which to scale this impenetrable fortress. In which case perhaps a ladder was in order. "I remember, and that is enough. You dropped me at the entrance of the village and told me to forget. Ironically enough, it was those words that stayed with me," said Michia, her eyes glistening.

"That is in the past," Greylancer said gruffly. "Your blood was warm and sweet, nevertheless. I am reborn. But perhaps I shall have another taste."

"Then please." His pale fingers twined around Michia's hand clutching the vials. She was frozen by the pain like steel wires digging into her flesh.

"Why must I drink such dregs when your hot lifeblood is so plentiful here?" Greylancer drew her into his arms. "My eyes can see the veins in your body. My ears can hear your blood flowing. My mouth yearns to drain it dry."

"My lord..." Michia moaned. Her eyes grew shrouded in mist. Hot breath escaped her lips. Under the tyrannical gaze of the oppressor, humans most often cringed and cowered and seethed. Perhaps Greylancer recognized that Michia was an exception. This woman showed none of the inescapable fear or hatred that his victims usually betrayed when under his spell. "How I have waited for this moment," she gasped. "Take me where you will. Turn me into whatever you please. It has long been my wish to die by your hand, ever since you rescued me when I was fifteen."

When she threw her arms against his chest, Greylancer faltered.

This was an uncommon experience for the brave and peerless warrior. That look of blatant terror on the victim's face just before the "kiss" was the one thrill a vampire existed for. Yet here was this woman throwing herself into his embrace.

Greylancer put a hand on her chin and gazed into her face. "Your kind have always looked into my eyes and could do little else but cower in terror. You are not like them. Are you not afraid of me?

"Why no," she answered, her voice dreamy. "Had you not

found me in that forest seventeen years ago, I would be an entirely different woman. You saved my life. It is yours to do with as you please."

Greylancer furrowed his brows. "Are you weeping?"

"I do not know." Another luminous tear rolled down her cheek.

"I don't understand it. The act of crying, that is. The Nobility have never shed tears. Nor have I. I have heard that humans cry for two reasons. Fear and sorrow. If you are not afraid, are you sad?"

"No." Michia shook her head. "I have cried out of sadness only once in my life, shortly after I was born. I have never wept since. That is the same for all humans on the Frontier."

"Why is that?"

"We have no time for tears if we want to live," answered Michia, looking away for a moment. "Half of the children die within two months of their birth. The land in these parts can barely grow a tenth of the crops that we need to survive."

"You receive necessary rations from the Administration Bureau in the Capital." Greylancer's tone turned serious. Overseeing the Northern Frontier sector was his responsibility.

For the first time, an incredulous expression came into Michia's eyes. "Do you not know?"

"About what?"

"The rations we receive from the Bureau do not last any of the villages more than a week."

"That's absurd. I've seen to it that you will never go hungry. Your welfare has always been a priority."

"But you do not deliver the supplies yourself."

"You're not suggesting—my vassals? Profiteering?" He shook his head. A ferocious gleam began to burn in his eyes. "Why do you weep now, amid this reality too hard for tears? And…"

Greylancer swallowed his words, as a faint smile crept across Michia's face.

"There is another reason why I weep," she said, hopeful and bashful at the same time.

"Speak it now," said Greylancer gravely.

Her pale arms twined around his neck.

It was a moment best described as a miracle.

No other time in history has a human, neither spellbound by a Noble's gaze nor seeking servitude, ever willingly desired a Noble.

"I weep because—" Michia stopped. Greylancer looked up at the entrance. "What's wrong?"

"An unfortunate intruder." Greylancer clenched Michia's hand.

Four silhouettes rushed inside and scattered about the stable.

"Michia—what are you *doing*?" The earth-scorching cry belonged to Chief Lanzi.

Though she let go of his hand, rather than pulling away, Michia collapsed over Greylancer's lap.

"What are...my lord, just what have I done to earn your disfavor?" The chief trembled violently.

Two of the men appeared to be the chief's hired hands, and the other, Greylancer recognized. The man had been the one glaring at Greylancer with murderous intent at the tavern.

"My lord...what is...this?" An emotion unlike despair and shock swelled in the chief's voice.

CHAPTER 3:
THE PRIVY COUNCIL'S
DECISION

1

Greylancer rose to his feet and offered no explanation in his defense. Resuming the bearing of an overlord ruling over his lowly human subjects, the Noble glared.

A shock wave of contempt and anger ripped through the four intruders. They were sent reeling on their heels, and two of the men fell onto their backsides.

"The door was open, so you are forgiven for not knocking or announcing your presence. I shall take my leave." Greylancer moved toward his cybernetic horse without so much as acknowledging Michia.

"My lord," said the voice of a younger man. When Greylancer did not slow his pace, the voice called out, "There's something you should see."

Sensing an odd confidence in the frightened voice, Greylancer turned his head.

A horrible chill stabbed like a stake at his immortal heart.

A youth of about twenty with his head wrapped in bandages stood clutching a rusty cross in his outstretched hand.

The others let out a cry. Though there were only four men including the chief, their voices rang across the stable with the force of an entire division of men.

"So it works," said the youth. "I was wandering around some

old religious ruins and came across an ancient tome. I guess what was written in it was true—the Nobility fear the crucifix." He nodded at the others behind him, but two of the men were paralyzed with fear, as the stakes and hammers trembled in their hands. "Don't just sit there! Do it!" yelled the youth at the top of his lungs.

"Chief, Chief…" Greylancer gnashed his teeth.

The chief was struck motionless by the fury in Greylancer's voice. The cross was supposed to render the Noble unconscious, or so the youth had said. But though the Noble had averted his eyes, he hardly appeared shaken, much less about to fall into a swoon.

Greylancer hulked over the chief like a mountain. "Have you any idea what you're doing?"

"I-I know it," stammered the chief. His teeth chattered as if to rebuke the temerity of his actions. "Th-this is an act for… for all humanity! A day that will live in history. This night will sound the starting shot of humanity's revolt against the Nobility!" The last words tripped off his tongue, not from growing calm but from desperate abandon.

Meanwhile the youth with the cross ran up to one of the feckless men on the ground and seized a stake and hammer. "Father!"

Chief Lanzi winced.

"Ah, so he is your son, is he? You also spoke of a daughter." Greylancer's voice took on a scornful tone that seemed to threaten not only Chief Lanzi but also his progeny in the present and extending into all eternity.

Lanzi's son shoved the two weapons to his father's chest. "Father, stab him in the heart with this."

The stake and hammer rattled in the chief's arms, as his entire body trembled.

"Father!" cried his son. But when Lanzi continued to shake, he yelled, "Then hold this. I'll end him!" The youth shoved the cross in his father's hands and took the stake and hammer in his own.

As he stood ready to lunge at Greylancer, Michia intervened for the first time. "Stop it, Lanok. You must stop. Lord Greylancer is—"

"I don't want to hear it!" cried Lanok. "You've been a good mother to us. You never hit us or threw us out in the dead of winter for disobeying you, like our real mother. You were fair, but firm, an ideal mother. Leticia and I have always thought of you as our real mother. But now, look at you! Throwing yourself into the arms of this Noble. You're a traitor! A traitor to Leticia, my father, and me, your friends, the village, the Frontier, and all of humanity! Leticia is lucky she isn't here to witness this. As soon as I finish the Noble, you're next!" These baleful words were enough to paint over the night with sorrow.

Lanok rushed forward with the stake pointed at Greylancer's chest and lifted the hammer over his head.

Tackling his side to intercept his advance was Michia.

The two tangled and spun around several times in the other's clutches before tumbling to the ground.

The cybernetic horses let out a loud whinny.

"Chief Lanzi," boomed Greylancer. "Put down the cross!"

The old chief dropped the crucifix as if he'd been struck by a thunderbolt.

Greylancer's right arm traced a wicked arc.

It was easy enough to call it a sudden flash of steel. But the tip of the lance exceeded three meters and its grip easily five meters in length.

The blade stopped not on Lanok, who'd scrambled to his feet, but at the throat of his companion, who was left twitching helplessly on the ground.

The Noble cast a smile that might rightly be called benevolent. With his eyes trained on the boy before him, Greylancer addressed the rebel leader. "Lanok, was it? As overseer, I have governed over this land by example. My regard for you humans is no different than that of other Nobles. But I will not promise your safety and leave you to fend for yourselves in a wasteland not even beasts or monsters dare inhabit. Nor will you be laid to slaughter for my gain. And in return my demand is this—absolute loyalty. It is easily given. Do not cross me, do not talk back in anger, and do not lie. And never raise a sword against me. They are the commandments I have passed down to you at my appointment and have repeated time and again. You have been allowed to live in peace ever since. A peaceful life. Is that not what you humans desire?"

"Ruled by the Nobility, surviving on what rations you toss our way—*peaceful*? Even if that were true, it's no way to live. We live and breathe! As long as we are subjugated by your rule, we might as well be dead. What good is living in death? There are enough living dead already! Cursed vampires, cold-blooded bastards! This planet was born for us warm-blooded humans!" Lanok shouted, "You will die proudly, Hendry!"

"Hmph, did you hear him," Greylancer said to the youth named Hendry. "A mere boy who must be defended by his mother. Will you listen to *him*?" The lance dug into the boy's throat. Blood snaked down his neck. "Tell me that you want to be saved. Cry and scream that you do not want to die. Grovel before me and beg for your life. Then you will be allowed to live. Then you shall have the honor of serving me."

When Hendry heard this, a certain look floated across his face. Lanok let out a groan.

A servant of the Nobility—a human who is bitten and dies by the hand of a Noble returns to life with the same abilities of the Nobility. As one of the living dead. A vampire. When he submits to his station as a well-heeled dog of his master, he ceases to be human. Most such servants would think of themselves as better than human.

A most sweet proposition. A delectable existence indeed. Those humans who joined the lowest ranks of the bloodstained world became informants and traitors against their brethren.

At that moment, a certain look came across the faces of these humans—one of terror, panic, guilt, and an avarice that exceeded all of the former. It was the very look that had crept across Hendry's face.

"Die, Hendry!" Lanok shouted again.

"No!" cried his friend. "I didn't want to pick a fight with the Nobles in the first place. You dragged me into this. I don't want to die. God knows I don't want my head torn off and tossed in the streets for crows and monsters to pick at." Hendry turned to Greylancer and continued, "Yes, make me your servant." Hendry turned over onto his knees and touched his forehead against the dirt.

"Very well." The giant came forward. Throwing back his cape, Greylancer grabbed Hendry by the hair, pointed his face upward, and buried his face in the boy's neck.

"Hendry!" Lanok let out a heartrending cry.

Soon anguish and an indelible look of rapture spread over Hendry's face. Lanok imagined the blood of another world pouring into his friend's veins.

Hendry's body convulsed violently.

Aside from the two crimson lines trickling down his throat, a bloody flower began to spread its petals over his chest. The tip of a deadly stake tore through the wool shirt and emerged from his chest.

"Vachss?"

As the others remembered the presence of another youth, the boy named Vachss drew back the stake he'd driven into his treacherous friend's heart from behind and swung for Greylancer's chest.

The spike had pierced through Greylancer's green and gold embroidered shirt and clear through his chest.

"Well done. So you are a lad with some courage." Greylancer glanced up at Vachss as he passed a free hand across Lanok's face, which was set in an indescribable expression. "Alas, too late. Your friend has already fallen prey to my kiss, and you will have to die. A most brutal death."

"Why...why...do you not fall?" Vachss's mouth opened and closed like that of a fish found in a market.

"Pray," said Greylancer. "Pray to the god you believe in. Or you will never destroy me."

Vachss had a god he believed in. He would not be able to endure this world otherwise. Though he tried to intone a prayer, memory failed him.

"I heard that if you pray from your soul, God will be by your side. And I am unable to lay a hand on him. I want to see this god. Pray."

The Noble's inexplicably solemn voice seemed to summon Vachss's memory.

Amid the stench of blood beginning to fill the stable.

"Lord…I will fear no evil…for thou art with me…" The others listened to the horribly arid voice that came haltingly at first and then turned into a desperate echo. "…the Lord is my shepherd…He maketh me to lie down in green pastures. He leadeth me beside the still waters."

Perhaps someone among them was aware that Vachss's god had been born in a manger. Were that the case, perhaps bearing witness to another birth in this stable did not seem strange.

Soon the prayer ended.

A pious calm pervaded the barn, like moonlight on the Holy Night.

"Do you see Him?" Vachss asked—of whom, it was not clear. Perhaps Greylancer, or Chief Lanzi.

"Y-yes…" The chief nodded. "He—"

"—is not here."

The instant Vachss recognized the voice belonging to Greylancer, his head twisted 360 degrees. The sound of his neck bones being crushed reverberated across the barn.

"What's the matter, Chief? Lanok?" After dropping the dead body atop the corpse of the other boy, Greylancer shot a look at Lanok standing dumbstruck. "So your god does not come, even when you give prayer. I must say I am disappointed."

The Noble's long lance howled once more, cutting a path for Chief Lanzi's neck.

His head sailed through the air in a gush of blood as the lance took aim at a new target.

Greylancer let slip a gasp.

Before the sidelong sweep of the lance could slice Lanok's chest in two, Michia had jumped out in front of her son. The blade was wedged halfway into her torso.

2

Greylancer stared down at the young mother as she fell to her knees in a spray of blood. This mortal wound was evidence of either a lack of skill or the Noble's singular ability to halt his lance mid-swing.

"Run," said Michia in a blood-gurgling voice, prompting the Noble to turn toward the young insurgent.

After being pushed to the ground again, Lanok recovered his feet and tried to go to where his mother lay.

"Don't—" Michia rasped. "Hurry, you must run."

Lanok whirled around and eyed the door behind him. "Mother."

"…quickly." Then Michia collapsed.

Lanok chose to do his mother's bidding.

As he let out a mournful wail and ran for the door, Greylancer pointed the lance at the boy's back.

"Don't."

The woman's thread-thin voice halted the bloodshed. When the Noble craned his neck downward, Michia was clinging to his right leg. Fresh blood trailed behind from where she had fallen and crawled. Blood that he had spilled.

Greylancer's face betrayed a look of confusion, perhaps for the first time in his life.

"You defended me and defended your son, and for that, you will die by my lance. Why? Why do you protect two enemies?"

"…neither is…an enemy…of…mine…"

The thread began to break.

"My lance will kill you. You protected your son, knowing this. You could have lived another day. Do you not value your life?"

"A life...which you once saved. I am...content...to be able... to do the same. It will take time for...my son...to understand... so do not forget...that I saved you...and Lanok."

"I will remember. You have my word," said Greylancer, surprised by his own heartfelt reply.

Michia collapsed and did not stir again.

"Now you are dead." Amid the stillness and stench of blood pervading the room, only the low murmur of Greylancer's voice drifted about. "You humans all die so quickly. Flesh decays, and bones are left to bleach and crumble away in the wind. Why do you die so quickly? Why do you give your life for others, knowing so? For your son, I understand. But why did you not hesitate to save mine?" Greylancer hoisted the lance high in the air and stared at the blade. "I have taken the life of one who protected mine."

If one's voice told the secrets of the soul, no doubt the Noble named Greylancer was harboring a certain emotion.

An emotion called grief.

†

Bistoria, the capital city of the Northern Frontier sector, was eternally dampened by fog and rain. The cities heavily populated by Nobility were deliberately designed to maximize shadows, where Nobles could amble down the stone-paved streets or otherwise rush past the gaslights in coaches.

What Greylancer found waiting for him upon his return from the Frontier was an order to report to the Capital at once.

This is sudden. What do they want? he mused to himself.

Quietly, Greylancer boarded the emergency aircraft. The flight to the Capital was three hours.

Inside the halls of the Privy Council Ministry, ten members

of the council, awaiting Greylancer's arrival, were discussing matters of the war against the OSB. Two members were not present. They had gone missing several days ago.

Moonlight flooded in from the narrowly cut windows, and flames flickered in the bronze candle holders affixed throughout the hall. The artificial lighting was more of a habit than a natural predilection of Nobles endowed with night vision.

"Any progress in developing the technology to detect the OSB transformations or to prevent them outright?"

"We haven't heard anything more from the Central Research Center."

"The attack against the enemy's moon base?"

"We've been systematically attacking the base with unmanned aerial vehicles and long-range missiles but have not been able to penetrate the enemy's upgraded barriers. The best course of action would be a manned attack exploiting any momentary tears in the barrier. Aside from wooden stakes and steel blades, the OSB have yet to discover any weapons we're not proof against. In hand-to-hand combat, we will be victorious. Their shape-shifting attacks will be ineffective against us. Even if they take another form, we will simply destroy everything in our path. Even their atomic cannons will be useless."

"What about signs of religious behavior? Both the Theological Institute and Phenomena Bureau report that if the OSB find spirituality, their god might be able to discover our weaknesses."

"We needn't concern ourselves just yet. Their religion has only achieved a penetration factor of twenty percent to eighty percent for a scientific worldview. It will take some time before they consider the supernatural."

"How long?"

"Perhaps a millennium."

"Hmph, the blink of an eye."

"Still, time enough to devise a strategy to annihilate the enemy. We need only blast a hole in the wall and send in the infantry. When their current deployment does not return, their home planet will think twice about invading this solar system. Then we shall only be too glad to return the favor."

"With regard to the war on this planet, what do you know about the number of OSB incursions, their incursion route, and rate of human transformation?"

"I'll answer in order. To date, there have been seven reported incursions within fifty kilometers of the Capital, all of which have been neutralized. Rather like parachuting into the middle of our military. Based on the knowledge acquired from the humans they assimilated, they naturally narrowed the incursion point to the Frontier. There have been sixty-six confirmed incursions this month. The four overseers reported that every invader had been neutralized, but given how members of the Statistics Bureau have been attacked in the field, no doubt many more OSB have infiltrated the Frontier and taken human form than have been reported."

"What are the overseers doing?"

"Overseeing the Frontier sectors carries with it difficulties unimaginable to those of us here in the Capital. Which is precisely the reason why the overseers have been given a wider reach of powers than we wield over the Capital."

"If it is a matter of competence, why do we not replace them?"

"The current overseers have achieved the highest success among any of their predecessors. None of the four are easily replaced."

"What about the trouble in the Western Frontier sector?"

"Are you referring to Mayerling? The South and East report that he has become too involved with the humans."

"Any reports from the North?"

"The Noble Greylancer." Silence enveloped the spacious hall as soon as the name was expelled into the air. "He has reported nothing. You're aware as well as I, he is not given to exposing the misdeeds of others."

"Indeed, he is a born warrior. Were he here, this war would not have lasted as long as it has. Though were he in command, every one of us would be sent to the front lines."

Another silence fell over the council members, one of universal agreement this time.

"No matter, he is presently in the Frontier. Now that these old bones have escaped being sent to the battlefield, let us lay out a strategy against the OSB, shall we?"

And then a synthetic voice announced, "Lord Greylancer is here."

As tumult rippled among the men, one of the council members finally looked upward. "Tell him we're engaged in an important meeting." No sooner had he said it than the door that could not be opened from the outside slid open, inviting the navy-caped figure inside.

"Noble Greylancer." One of the men uttered the name that the others shouted silently to themselves.

"What urgent matter is this? Whatever your business, see that you call first."

After waiting for the councilor to finish, Greylancer paid what respect he could muster and gave the men a perfunctory bow. "I come in response to *your* summons. The Privy Council's transport brought me here directly from the airport. The driver handed me a pass, which is how I gained entry here."

"Who would do such a thing?" shouted a councilor. No doubt the same question echoed in all their minds. All except one.

"That would be me."

All of the eyes, including Greylancer's, gathered on the owner of the voice.

The voice belonged to the old man seated in the chancellor's chair at the far end of the long marble table.

Though he wore the same night-colored gown as the others, only his tiny sandaled feet stuck out from the translucent reddish-blue ball of liquid in which he was encased.

"Chancellor Cornelius."

"But what possessed you to act alone in this way?"

"If I'd consulted you, the answer would have been obvious. I've prepared my resignation. You will have it in due time." Each time the old man spoke, bubbles burbled out of his mouth. It was a peculiar sight, like seeing an aged infant floating in amniotic fluid inside the womb.

"State your business," Greylancer said calmly, though it was clear to anyone that he would turn on his heel and leave in a second were he told he had been summoned without good reason.

"Tomorrow, an unprecedented number of OSB fighters will descend upon this world from their lunar base. We received a message last night that you are the only one who can intercept this attack and destroy the enemy's moon base."

Greylancer felt his body stiffen.

The chancellor of the Privy Council said he'd received a message. *From whom?*

Looking calmly around at the men frozen like stone statues, Chancellor Cornelius continued, "My aides have made the necessary preparations. Dawn will break in little more than four hours. Your chariot awaits."

"As you command." Greylancer pressed an arm against his chest and bowed deeply. "However, I question the wisdom of giving me sole command of the counterstrike force. General Gaskell of the First Air Chariot Battalion, General Brewster of the Second Battalion, and General Nombusol of the Third Battalion are giants of uncommon ability. Taking command over them…" The thought hung in the air.

The Air Chariot Battalion buzzed like a swarm of crane flies around the saucer-shaped airship bristling with gun barrels.

As soon as the dimensional conversion wave crashed against the enemy's barrier, a white tear appeared in the air. But only for a moment before quickly disappearing, making the enemy impervious to attack again.

"Ah, if only crushing them were *this* easy," boomed a voice from above. An enormous hand knocked down the enemy airship along with the chariots.

The place was the Capital, in the War Ministry's spacious meeting room. Like the Privy Council Ministry, the room was enveloped in moonlight and blue darkness.

The five generals of the Air Chariot Battalions were seated at various sofas some distance apart from the others; to anyone aware of the discord among them, they might have appeared to be a hundred meters apart.

They all wore khaki-colored capes identifying them as military and held staves bearing the commander's insignia: a golden bat. What was most eye-catching, however, was the chain of fire clusters hanging from their necks.

True to their name, these nuggets of flame were burning replicas of fixed stars burning at six million degrees. They were medals awarded by the Privy Council for valor and victory in battle. Over a hundred such clusters hung from the five men's chains, threatening neither to scorch their skin nor melt their garments. They were shielded in a dimensional barrier, shunting the six-million-degree heat into another universe, so that it might never touch the wearer's cape a mere centimeter away.

Even one Sun Medal would earn a warrior the title of hero. The Noble army was teeming with foot soldiers with more than a hundred such medals, surpassing the records of even these generals.

Medals for the brave.

No society carried out this practice more diligently than the Nobility.

"The enemy's barrier grows more powerful by the day. They refuse to be satisfied by the success of the previous day. Our military can learn from their example." The giant standing two meters tall touched the air with a finger. An OSB airship ten times larger than the previous incarnation floated up in the void. "But we have finally succeeded in creating a dimensional cutter capable of cutting a tear into their barrier." The giant's finger made a slash mark across the flank of the enemy ship. The ship tore in half along the mark and burst into flames.

"Any complaints, Nombusol?" The tall man in the bi-horn helm growled and drank from the gold cup in his hand. He wiped the liquid from his mouth with the back of a hand. Blood. The contents of the others' cups were the same, as was fitting for a gathering of vampires.

"All is easier said than done, Brewster." General Nombusol answered proudly as if he'd found a comrade's error. "The reality is the cutter is barely capable of creating a tear in the new barrier and will not be able to do any damage on the airship or moon base. It will come down to a ground attack."

"Hence the reason why the Nobility's bravest have been secretly chosen for this counteroffensive. The matter cannot be left to androids."

"The OSB have full knowledge of the extent of our resources. Surely you haven't forgotten how our android soldiers turned against us in the assault before last. What this counteroffensive requires are flesh-and-blood warriors seething with the will to achieve victory and a thrill for carnage."

"Then I suggest you hand over command to me," said General Vilzen, seated closest to the entrance. His entire face was silver. Roughly hewn slits for the eyes and mouth. A mask. Ever since the generals here first encountered Vilzen in his youth, he had worn the same mask, albeit a different size. They could only surmise that his face had been terribly disfigured. No rumor or consensus on the matter existed, as anyone who initiated such rumor perished. "My three hundred Sun Medals are second to none. The enemies I have felled exceed five thousand. Surely, it is I the OSB fear most."

"An impressive number. The same number of fatalities you've incurred, I might add," sneered the white-haired man sitting farthest away by the window. Despite his white mane, the childlike face and high-pitched voice revealed this Noble's relative youth. It was what was commonly called a tinny voice. Yet the staff in his hand strangely suited him. "Indeed, you have disposed of over five thousand of the enemy. However, it is your methods that I take issue with. They were effective in recklessly shooting down the OSB airships. But while you were onto the next target before finishing off the first, the OSB crash landed on Earth and massacred humans on the ground. To date, roughly ten thousand Nobles on the Frontier have perished at the hands of the OSB, a third of those fatalities brought about by your slipshod command. No, I shall take command of this counteroffensive."

"Damn you, Minsky." Vilzen rose to his feet, his mask refracting the moonlight like sparks.

"That's enough, both of you," said another voice, one hoarse like that of a man on his deathbed. The wizened old man had arrived first and had been nodding off in the chair beneath the moonlight when the other generals arrived. One touch—or breath—might rend him in pieces. Yet his eyes, now open, emanated an eerie glint that froze the others. "General Brosius." He mumbled his name through his gums, not because he was senile or because the other four had forgotten his name. He did so partly in jest and in part to intimidate.

Hopping out of the chair, he tottered forward like a drunkard and approached the large table. "I'm not yet awake. I would have preferred never to wake. Perhaps you will help me."

He waved his staff.

Another miniaturized figure of an OSB airship appeared in the air. Unlike the blue and white schematic that Nombusol had produced, this one was a full-color, three-dimensional model—an exquisitely rendered miniature.

Crimson rays blasted out of its gun barrels.

Atomic beams. One shot through Old Brosius's face and flashed a brilliant ball on his right shoulder and fizzled.

Another beam obliterated Brewster's face from the nose up. A ball of light appeared on the right side of Nombusol's chest. Another on the left of Minsky's chest. More beams shot holes through the ceiling and floor.

"Now I'm awake." There was a gaping hole in the middle of Old Brosius's face, the view behind him visible through the hole in his face. When he tapped the holographic airship with the staff, the hole disappeared.

"A most rude awakening," grumbled Nombusol, the hole in his chest already mended.

"Now where is Gaskell?" Old Brosius regarded the men and asked.

"He went to the western outskirts on reconnaissance last night and was shot down. A rescue squadron has been dispatched, but nothing, at present, is known about his whereabouts or safety." It was Vilzen who answered.

"Safety aside, his whereabouts are something of a concern. Could he have been taken captive?"

"Knowing him, he would rather drive a stake into his own heart before having to endure the shame of capture," said Minsky. "Simple man that he is." The general grinned, though not so much out of respect for Gaskell's sensibilities.

"One less general suits me fine." Nombusol bared his teeth and smiled. "So there are three candidates. And I shall include myself."

"And I," said Brewster, rapping his staff against his left hand.

Smiling, Old Brosius said, "Surely, an election will not do. You will all attempt to eliminate the opposition and then cast a vote for yourselves. In the first place, I find it odd the Privy Council has not yet appointed a commander."

"Does the Council have a candidate in mind?" Minsky asked, his fangs gnashing.

No doubt the other generals present wanted to do likewise. The Air Chariot Battalion was an elite group chosen from the Nobility's best warriors. Immortal as the Nobles were, they all varied by disposition. There were brave ones, and then there were cowards. Though the matter of training was left up to the individual, every last Noble with an aggressive disposition recognized himself a warrior and entered the Capital's Training Center.

It was at the Center that Nobles were sorted and tested on their aptitude as warriors based on three factors: physical ability, self-possession, and belligerence. While this was comparable to humanity's conscription system, whether these Nobles chose to become warriors and continue more advanced combat training was up to the individual.

Despite the incongruity of immortal beings serving on the battlefield, the Nobility had gained complete knowledge of supernatural phenomena known as the occult even before they gained supremacy over the world.

Phenomena that humanity had disdained as nonsense and child's play had revealed themselves as unmistakable truths. Among them was the existence of unidentified flying objects—UFOs.

That UFOs, long considered nothing more than optical phenomena, had been aggressively engaged in infiltrating the planet was kept confidential among the world's governments. The human world established an investigative agency, which concluded the UFOs were not merely engaged in observation but laying the foundation for invasion.

The Nobility had inherited that knowledge.

The enemy from outer space will someday bare its teeth and attack.

The Nobility prepared for this threat and developed weapons that took into account the distinct advantages of their immortality.

They also concentrated their efforts into their defenses so they could protect physical assets such as the Capital.

Thanks to advances in modern weaponry, hand-to-hand combat had been rendered all but obsolete. But the Nobility had resisted modernity tooth and nail.

Despite preserving the nuclear weapons once eschewed by humanity, plus an arsenal of antiproton cannons, dimensional oscillators, and DNA-destroying viruses they'd devised in the course of their war against the OSB, the Nobility deemed these weapons as last-resort methods to be deployed only in the face of wholesale slaughter and defeat. They instead concentrated the bulk of their efforts on antiquated military tactics.

Their plan was to destroy the OSB's defenses, breach the lunar base, and then annihilate the enemy in hand-to-hand combat.

Imprinted in the Nobility's DNA was a deep nostalgia for the past, as a bird's-eye view of the Noble world so plainly made evident. That they insisted on adhering to the ways of antiquity even on the battlefield might best be attributed to their psyche.

If winning victory by plunging a sword, an arrow, a spear into the enemy was the measure of valor, then the Air Chariot Battalion was rightly the Nobility's most elite group, and its commanders had earned universal respect as the best of the best warriors.

Thus the prospect of a newcomer taking over the reins of command was hardly news generals would welcome.

"Perhaps an errant shot of the antiproton cannon might encourage the Privy Council to reconsider," said Nombusol, echoing what was surely on the minds of the others. Yet his suggestion was only met with silence.

Even dauntless generals of the likes of Brewster and Old Brosius glanced up at the sky as if fearing someone had heard.

"Hold your tongue, Nombusol!" said Old Brosius, making certain to utter the blasphemer's name clearly. "The high chancellor of the Privy Council—he is the Sacred Ancestor."

The face of the brazen general turned ashen.

CHAPTER 4:
CRIMSON SONG

1

"Then..." Minsky pressed his hands against his twitching cheeks. "The commander was handpicked by the Sacred Ancestor himself? No, could it be..."

No...

No...

No...

Could it be...

Could it be...

Could it be...

A red wind gusted into the generals' hearts.

Blowing away sand and rock, the wind surfaced a rumor they'd forcibly kept hidden and dared not contemplate.

The Sacred Ancestor has a son.

It existed in a realm of consciousness beyond the reach of thought. Only rumor, which none were allowed to touch, dwelled there.

Suddenly, the bronze door opened, putting an end to the intractable chaos.

The men blinked at the shadow at the door and cried out at once.

Greylancer!

The self-righteousness swelling inside the generals turned to dust and vanished.

It was the moment they acknowledged the presence of the one warrior that eclipsed them all.

"The Six Demon Generals—it has been a long time," said Greylancer, his voice dripping with disdain rather than nostalgia. The Nobility's vaunted generals were little more than callow recruits in his eyes. Looking down at the paralyzed men, he said dispassionately, "Gaskell is not here—perished, has he?" and continued, "By order of the Privy Council, I will take command of tomorrow's attack on the OSB moon base. I expect nothing less than your full efforts." Giving them not a moment to object, Greylancer ran a hand across the air. "Here is the plan."

An image of the moon ten meters in diameter appeared before him.

†

"We proceed as planned. Go," said Greylancer as his chariot picked up speed. Was this some kind of fantasy or fairy tale?

The Greater Noble's vehicle, racing through space toward Earth's moon, was none other than a wheeled chariot from human antiquity.

Flying close behind was a fleet of aircraft, all with wings arched like those of bats.

The Nobility had previously attempted several attacks against the OSB frontline base on the far side of the moon three hundred thousand kilometers from Earth but had only managed to delay the OSB infiltration of Earth, a fact that made the temples of the Privy Council members pulse with rage.

None of the allied aircraft's propulsion nozzles were lit; an antigravitational propulsion field surrounding each of the craft propelled them forward instead.

Perhaps having foreknowledge of the imminent invasion, the OSB commenced their attack. Soon golden laser beams crisscrossed this way and that around the fleet.

"Atomic cannons. If you go down, wait on the lunar surface for the rescue vessel," Greylancer ordered.

A beam shot at Greylancer's chariot—and was refracted away as if skipping off an invisible spherical surface.

When the fleet came within three thousand kilometers of the moon, a swarm of OSB aircraft rose up from the surface.

"Move to single combat maneuvers. When you've destroyed your target, after me."

A human field general typically directed operations from the rear. But a Noble of any mettle *led* his men into battle.

The attack order was not "Forward," but "After me." These were Greylancer's chosen words.

Noblesse oblige—the obligation borne by humans of high birth, royalty and nobility, in return for their high ranking. Driven by this obligation, the Nobility always stood at the vanguard of their fleet. Cowards were they that shouted "Forward!" from a position of safety. Noble warriors simply said, "After me," and were the first to draw weapons fire.

And so too did the Nobility's greatest warrior. But were not Nobles immortal? No, the enemy's primary weapon was not the atomic cannon but what followed.

The OSB fired a spread of graviton spheres. When they came into contact with Noble aircraft, they neutralized the antigravitational propulsion field. One after the next, the ion engines of the bat-shaped aircraft flamed on.

The atomic cannon followed, destroying the aircraft. Then, as the jettisoned pilots plummeted through space, a barrage of stakes and steel arrows rained down to impale them.

Greylancer threaded his chariot past the spheres, destroyed them as he passed, and closed in on the moon base.

The feeling of movement was imperceptible in gravitational field propulsion. No matter how fast he spun, aside from the visual change, Greylancer was incapable of perceiving three-dimensional movement from within his chariot.

"Do not fail me, rear squadron."

A peculiarly shaped spherical building encircled by rings came into view ahead.

The antiproton cannons affixed on either side of the chariot poured hot beams into the barrier shielding the building.

The antiproton beam was capable of vaporizing protons and all matter in existence.

Yet the beams glanced off the barrier wall and only vaporized the unlucky OSB craft in the vicinity.

It was a deadly gamble. Would the Military Bureau's dimensional cutter on Earth be able to disrupt the enemy's barrier from three hundred thousand kilometers away?

If the cutter failed, Greylancer would fly into the barrier and be reduced to dust. And if the cutter were even a thousandth of a second off, Greylancer would be banished to another dimension.

The Greater Noble did not flinch and pointed the chariot toward the barrier.

Was it his split-second evasive skills he trusted? The Military Bureau's invention? Or his own luck?

The barrier tore open.

As the chariot plunged into the white one-by-three-kilometer tear in the dimension, the antiproton stream reversed direction and the vortex dragged Greylancer's craft down onto the lunar surface, right into the OSB's base.

†

Inside the oddly shaped building there existed silver-colored automatons. Having no natural shape of their own, the OSB had created organic beings by forming and discarding body parts, then stitching the disparate anatomies together. The patchwork beings were designed to carry out simple tasks. In parallel, the OSBs developed new and upgraded incarnations of robots until finally, combining the two offspring populations, they perfected organisms that might best be called cybernetic beings.

Then the protean OSBs adopted the form of their own cybernetic creations and gave rise to a unique civilization.

The OSB appeared to possess a curiosity rivaling that of any other intelligent beings in the universe.

It was only a matter of time before they ventured into the ocean of constellations. In fact, the imminent destruction of their mother planet had made the endeavor all but imperative. As their sun began to expand due to an abnormal nuclear fusion and threatened to engulf the mother planet, the OSB devoted five thousand years to the construction of a massive space fleet. Resting their fates in the stars, they set out for another realm. Tens of thousands of years later, their wandering journey ended with the capture of a lone space probe.

After thoroughly researching its mechanism, the OSB decided to set course for the star system that produced this probe. Their intent was not peaceful coexistence but invasion and conquest. Domination. *Uncharted* was just another word for *wild*. Civilizing the wild in their own image—such was the mission their god had appointed them. They were forgiven any means to carry it out.

However, this would take another millennium. Although the OSB had developed a form of lightspeed technology, they discovered a habitable planet en route to the probe's birthplace and settled there.

They required no longer than a hundred years to make this planet their new home. The OSB slaughtered every extant species, and a strange civilization—one that began as amorphous creatures and later took the form of cyborgs—was born.

The OSB seemed fated to solitude. Scientists concluded that, despite enjoying a period of great prosperity, their civilization would become more isolated and eventually perish. The neighboring star systems were devoid of intelligent life. There were no species left to conquer.

Plagued by pangs of existentialism, the OSBs redirected their attention to the now-legendary probe and the distant stars.

Thus, with a hundred billion stars reflecting in the bodies of their aircraft, they embarked on a millennium-long journey of conquest.

By the time they entered Earth's solar system, however, the

Nobility were already aware of their existence. Anticipating an invasion from outer space, the Nobility had spread an elaborate surveillance network of satellites and planetoid bases throughout the star system.

The first skirmish broke out somewhere near Pluto.

Though the Nobility's fleet was crushed by the awesome firepower of the OSB, the existence of the Nobility struck fear in the invaders.

Why? Blown into space, the Noble warriors neither froze nor suffocated, but vanished into the void. After entering Pluto's orbit, five hundred or so Nobles had drifted around the planet until being rescued.

The second battle unfolded in Saturn's orbit, but despite an eventual retreat, the Nobility had dealt a great blow to the OSB.

Made to reckon with an uncommon foe, the OSB deployed an advance detachment to Earth.

By possessing the humans they encountered, the OSB obtained intelligence on their vampire enemies. They were astounded to learn of the Noble gift of immortality.

Meanwhile, the vampires captured an unfortunate OSB that had stolen the identity of a Noble.

Predicting an even fight in a battle of brute force, the OSB built a permanent base on the far side of the moon in anticipation of a war of attrition. Because they subsisted by altering their form to absorb any nearby energy sources, they required nothing more than solar energy while in their lunar bivouac.

Thus began the war between the OSB and Nobility that would span three thousand years.

2

The moon base was wrapped in silence. No audible alarm was necessary to alert an army of robots, nor was there air to carry any sound to a Noble's ears.

Robots on combat vehicles sped down the corridors, and fighters swooped down from above.

Gravitational field spheres flew about in every direction. The enemy intended to neutralize Greylancer's antigravitational field before unleashing an attack.

"I'm going in. Anyone who is able, after me!" Greylancer shouted. He moved to switch off the chariot's field.

"Commander, you mustn't do anything rash!" a voice said from the image of the console floating next to his ear. The two-dimensional grid contained all of the ship's controls within easy reach. "You will be cannon fodder if you lower your ship's field."

"Yunus." Greylancer muttered the name of his subcommander. "I can't be bothered to turn the field on and off. Only those that can need follow."

Robots armed with shoulder-mounted blade-launchers flanked the Noble and fired.

Greylancer dropped the field and reached for his lance.

He swung the massive weapon, and several explosions erupted in the vacuum around him. When the blades traveling at supersonic speed made contact with the lance, the convergence of the two opposing forces disintegrated the blades. Blue electromagnetic waves and ash scattered everywhere.

At what speed was such a feat possible? With what force? How do you track each blade and strike it down, Greylancer?

A rain of black arrows fell from the inky sky. The robots faithfully executed the legendary Earthian tactic for slaying vampires, only their arrows traveled at thirty-four kilometers per second.

Greylancer stood against each and every arrow shot at him. How exquisite, how awesome was the flash of his lance. And the arrows reversed their courses.

The arrows shot through the robots' faces, heads, and torsos, and felled one robot after the next, tendrils of blue lightning lashing out from their failing bodies.

Before he realized it, Greylancer was alone in the skies.

There were metal walls to the right and left of him that

cascaded down like waterfalls into the darkness below. He could not see bottom, as the chariot's console was not registering a measurement.

At the outset of the attack, Noble chariots had released nano-sized sensor insects to gather information on the base.

Greylancer's target was the energy core. The chariot's computer system was supposed to guide him there based on the intelligence gathered by the sensor insects.

The console projected in the the air read:

Distance to target converted to Noble measurement: 24,986 floors down.

More enemy aircraft approached. They numbered over a hundred. An object resembling a sphere with a stabilizer mounted on it unleashed a storm of blades and stakes.

The chariot repelled the attack and, powered by its ion engines, dropped in a straight line into the abyss at seventeen kilometers per second.

The g forces crushed Greylancer's face and nearly tore away his hair.

Countless red lights blipped on the console, in radar-mode.

Here they come. Greylancer's wind-twisted lips curled all the more. He was smiling.

The enemy dispersed.

After downing the blizzard of blades and stakes head-on, Greylancer rapped his knuckles against the handrail.

"Let us go somewhere they will not expect."

The robots repositioned themselves just as their computers directed, their formation aligning with how Greylancer routinely engaged multiple enemies. They placed unqualified trust in the analysis the computer extrapolated from an unfathomable number of scenarios.

But a full-frontal charge—

An impossibly long lance came at the robots from an impossible angle and plunged into their power units.

The lance laid waste to the aircraft too, sending them spiraling down as if they were chasing after a foe that had momentarily broken through the line.

This destruction, brought about by Greylancer's dreadful design, wrought even more devastation on the OSB.

The aircraft plummeted right into the path of the OSB infantry's counterattack. The volley of blades and stakes struck and bounced off the falling, flaming aircraft, virtually shielding Greylancer from the brunt of the attack. The chariot's antigrav field went back up and filled with air.

"Distance to target?"

The answer flashed across the console. *No change.*

Greylancer furrowed his brows, seemingly confused by the computer's answer. Whether a hundred thousand floors or a million floors below ground, at this speed he should be upon the energy core by now.

"What is it—a space warp?"

Negative. The target is mobile.

The power core is moving…? Greylancer thought, and then a flash of inspiration. "The moving walls…so the entire interior of the base is repositioning at supersonic speed. Counterstrategy?"

Increase velocity. The target's velocity is fifty kilometers per second.

"So it dares outrun this Noble?" He smiled a devilish smile, both beautiful and bloodcurdling. "Accelerate to fifty point five kilometers per second."

Affirmative. However, the combustion chamber will exceed heat capacity.

"The result?"

Explosion.

"Do it."

Fool.

In 0.5 seconds, the chariot's rate of descent surpassed that of the walls.

A green diagram glowed on the console.

It was a schematic of the base.

One point in the center pulsed red.

Greylancer's eyes glimmered scarlet. He had found the target.

Target acquisition in two seconds.

"Fifty-five kilometers per second."

Affirmative. The mechanized voice sounded appalled.

Greylancer's body groaned under the pressure brought on by the g forces. He felt his ribs snap and stab his internal organs. Greylancer coughed up blood. The force felt as if he were being crushed beneath a hundred-ton boulder.

Gradually, the chariot leveled off, and at the same time his bones healed. The organs inside his body regained function. It was evidence of why Nobles were Nobles.

One hundred thousand kilometers to target.

Greylancer read the message off the console and said, "Dimensional vortex shot. Just one shot."

Affirmative. Escape route secured. However, probability of escape is one percent.

"That's plenty. Fire!"

In the next instant, darkness filled his vision.

The dimensional shot—a weapon that not only destroys the target but also banishes the debris to another dimension—had dragged its handler into another world as well.

†

He was conscious and clear-headed.

Exactly eight seconds passed before the darkness dissipated. The scene that appeared in its place was a familiar one.

White clouds drifted across the blue sky. Greylancer stared pensively at the verdant foothills spreading in the distance. To the right of where he lay face up on the grass was the chariot, careened and battered.

Daytime. Though the time inside the vortex had *felt* like eight seconds, at least half a day appeared to have passed.

"No, perhaps days, or months."

At least the time of year seemed to be the same. The soft rays

of late autumn shone down on the Noble and on the chariot
next to him.

"Day…"

Greylancer passed the time as he'd done many times before,
lying perfectly still, looking up at the blue sky as if it were the
first he'd ever seen. A faint scent tickled his nostrils.

Several minutes passed before he realized something was amiss.
"What?"

Greylancer tried to twist his body to stand. Nothing. His
arms and legs remained motionless.

He could still move his eyes. His arms were fine, as well as
his legs.

But he seemed longer from the waist down. He fixed a hard
stare below. His waist and legs lay cold and lifeless an arm's
length away from the rest of his body.

The grass around him was drenched in blood. His blood.

"I can't move. So now what?" Greylancer gnashed his teeth,
frustrated by the unsightly damage to his frame. Was the battle on
the moon still going on? If so, he was useless, helpless. His pride
as a warrior forbade him from accepting this reality. "Someone
come this way. Kneel before me so I may satisfy my craving and
regain my freedom."

With this utterance, he heard footsteps approaching from
his left.

The sound of slow, tiny steps treading over the grass sounded
like a woman was coming near.

Greylancer did not let out a sound. What was he to do? It
appeared he would have to rely on human help, but what if the
sight of him as he was now fomented vengeful thoughts? Though
possessing an ample sense of superiority over his subjects, he
hardly underestimated them.

Before he could gather his thoughts, the footsteps stopped
before where Greylancer lay.

Her hair, hanging down to her waist, sparkled in the wind.
Although her pink dress with a blue-flower pattern was patched

and washed-out, it suited her as if she could wear nothing else.

She might have been fifteen, sixteen years old. Her pale skin, with nary a trace of color from the summer sun, was a fitting complement to her lovely features, which did not appear at all provincial.

But it was not the girl's beauty that made Greylancer's eyes narrow into slivers.

With her right hand gripping a stick, the girl was looking nervously right and left, her eyes closed.

"Can you not see?" They were the first words Greylancer uttered to the girl.

Her face turned toward him. "Who are you? You aren't from around here."

"How can you tell?"

"Your accent is different."

It is said the other senses become sharper in the blind, a necessity for survival.

"Hm. I am a traveler. I'm…resting my legs awhile."

"Oh, you've come to just the place."

"Yes, the view seems very nice."

The girl tilted her head slightly. "*Seems*…are you blind as well?"

Finally, a question came to his lips. "What brings you here?"

"I came to admire the view," she answered innocently, to which Greylancer responded, "But you do not see."

"I can see even if I can't. I can feel how the wind brushes against my skin, and the smell of flowers and grass fills my chest. My brother tells me the sky is blue, and that is enough for me to see. Everything. But you must see so much better than I."

"I'm afraid I'm too tired to move."

"Oh. Are you hungry?"

"That may be," replied Greylancer, as the blood continued to drain out of him.

"Oh…" The girl knitted her brows with worry before quickly smiling. "Someone will come to fetch me in half an hour. Then perhaps you can come to my home."

"Sadly, I have rather a particular palate. Your meals won't do."

"Well." The girl pouted a bit, but her anger faded quickly. Her sunny face revealed that this was just her personality. "Then what is it you eat?"

"Would you like to know?"

"Yes." A look of trepidation spread across her beautiful face. Just what had she sensed from the traveler's reply?

"Come closer." Greylancer's eyes glowed crimson, as the sweet bouquet of blood wafted in his face.

3

The severed lower half of the giant's body lay in a pool of blood, beckoning the other half to come closer.

The sight was enough to make even the most fearless human choose retreat.

Nevertheless, the blind girl began to walk toward Greylancer without even the slightest hint of hesitation. Despite her likely sharpened sense of smell, the stench of blood did not reach her upwind.

Aided by her stick, the tiny figure, hot blood coursing through its veins, crept closer, ever closer.

She stepped forward again, and as one wooden shoe hovered over the pool of blood—

"Stop," Greylancer said.

"Huh?" The girl teetered but managed to bring back her foot next to the other.

"Never you mind. Go now."

"But…" The girl's face clouded.

"It will soon turn cold. Go back to your home."

"Will you be all right?"

"Yes, I am rested now."

Like a stone turned to a flower, her suspicious look instantly gave way to a smile. "I'm glad," she said. "But I'm not to leave until my companion comes for me. Perhaps we can talk awhile."

"You must leave now!" His voice was stern. Greylancer was fighting back fierce urges.

The smell of his own blood around him stung his nostrils. It was what his enervated body was craving. Fresh blood. The one thing that will save you, and it was flowing through the young body standing before you.

Yet why did he stop?

The girl, clinging to her stick with both hands, gazed down in the direction of the voice with unsighted eyes. "My name is Leticia. Who are you?"

"No one you need concern yourself about."

The heartbroken girl—Leticia—pouted a little and then smiled. "Then you'll be Mr. No-Name. Where did you come from?"

"From the other side of the planet."

"*This* planet?" she asked, after a pause. "My, you *have* been on a long journey! Tell me, what is the other side like?"

"What day and month is it now?" asked Greylancer. After she answered, he muttered to himself, "A day has passed. Does the war continue above?"

"What?"

"Never you mind. Have you heard anything about the moon?"

"The moon…?" The girl thought for a moment. Then her blond hair rippled as she bobbed her head in the affirmative. "I heard a rumor that the Nobility's fleet destroyed the OSB base. In celebration of this victory, our blood tribute has been decreased by a tenth."

"Is that so?" Greylancer felt his fatigue dissipate, knowing his immediate return was not necessary.

Crooking her head, the girl asked, "But why would you ask about the moon? Oh, I know. You must be a troubadour!"

"Troubadour?"

"How wonderful. I've always wanted to meet one—someone who travels the world composing songs, that is. I never imagined it would be today. You must come home with me, please. Well, it's not exactly *my* home, but my mother and father are nice people.

They so enjoy having visitors, they will be glad to see you."

"Will they, now?"

"Yes." Leticia nodded eagerly like a child.

Seeing this, Greylancer asked, "Have you been blind since birth?"

She seemed taken aback by the question. "What—no. Since I was five." Until then, the world had shined for her.

"Are you bitter?"

"Why, of course."

"You surprise me."

"Why is that?"

"I have asked others in your state .the same question. They all answered no."

"I understand some people feel that way. But I…" A glimmer rolled down from the hand over her eye.

"What is it?" Greylancer asked and was surprised by his own reaction. *Have I taken an interest in a human?*

"I used to see the sky, the moon, the stars, flowers and the forest, animals, houses, and everyone. I used to see everything, until suddenly…I would have been happier had I been blind at birth." Then, Leticia shook her head, her body trembling. "I'm sorry. Prattling on to a complete stranger, I wonder why. I'm sorry for boring you."

"No." Greylancer stared at the troubled girl. Who would have guessed that a Noble was capable of looking upon a human with such kindly eyes? "It was an inconsiderate question. Forgive me."

"Please don't trouble yourself. I'm used to it."

"Have you tried every possible means?" he asked.

"It's all right." The girl smiled cheerfully.

"It is not. There may be a cure if you go to the Capital."

"Are you saying that I should have an operation at the hands of the Nobility?"

"That's right. The Nobility have the means to restore your sight, even reproduce the same eyes you previously had." The pale-skinned beauty smiled sadly this time. "What is it?"

Her lovely hands covered both eyes. "It was a Noble who took my sight."

"Oh…was it your overseer?"

"Perish the thought!" Leticia shook her head wildly. "You must never say such a thing. Lord Mayerling looks after us with great care. I don't know any Noble who is more decent."

"Mayerling…" The Greater Noble mumbled the name of his comrade in a barely audible voice. "That favormonger. Nevertheless, just my fortune that I've landed in his territory. He will have to receive me as a guest if he wants to repay his debts."

"What was that?"

"Nothing. Who was the Noble that took your sight?"

"I was given away for adoption as a girl. My real family didn't have the means to bring up a worthless girl like me. But I became this way because a neighboring family fled the village to join the Anti-Nobility Alliance. They were captured by the overlord's men and brought back to the village to be executed. Are you familiar with execution by quartering?"

"I know it. The condemned's neck, arms, and legs are chained to wagons and rended apart." Greylancer imagined the gruesome scene and licked his lips in spite of himself. The bloodbath.

The girl, none the wiser, lowered her gaze and recalled the incident. "The people who fled were not the only ones to be executed. Their actions wrought the same fate on their families, among them a young man who often looked after me as a child. I clung to him as he was being dragged to the execution ground. That was when the overlord's retainer lashed his whip across my eyes. I've lived in darkness ever since."

"A hard fate. The Noble who took your sight will suffer a death a hundred times more cruel than that of your friend."

"Don't talk like that." The girl shook her head, shaking off tears from her eyes and cheeks. "I've had enough with death and hurt. The Nobility may think nothing of being dismembered, but we humans must die screaming and crying in agony."

"Hm," Greylancer mused, looking down at his severed lower half.

"I'm sorry, I've only just met you. My emotions have gotten the best of me. I just thought that a bard might understand so many things." Wiping away the tears, Leticia said, "Perhaps you'll compose for me a song."

"A song?"

"Yes."

"First, answer me this. Who was the overseer that robbed you of your sight?"

"It was Lord Greylancer."

A cool wind brushed across the prairie. Waves of grass rippled where Greylancer lay. "Leticia…" he muttered. "Answer me another. You don't sound angry. Do you not bear a grudge against this overlord?"

"He did not order this man to take my sight from me."

"Yes, but—"

"But there is not enough anger in this world to express what I feel for the man who did this to me. If ever I found his grave, I would stop at nothing to drive a stake into his heart. But I bear no resentment toward the overlord."

"This overlord aside, do you not resent the Nobility?"

"My mother taught me that fate is the messenger of both happiness and misfortune."

"Your mother…? She abandoned you, did she not?"

"It was the only way they could survive. My mother and father held my hand and cried, time and again, over how sorry they were."

"Is parting always so sorrowful?"

"You must be a fortunate man to ask such a question. I'm glad."

"Glad?"

"Yes, I'm glad that people like you exist. I'm glad to have met you."

Greylancer directed his eyes away from her smile and looked up. A clear moon was now visible in the darkening blue sky. Only the day before, he'd been engaged in a vicious battle on the far side of the moon, and now he lay in a field on his home planet three hundred thousand kilometers away.

By his side stood a blind girl who told him she was happy they met.

"What else did your mother teach you?"

"Nothing will come of blaming fate. That I am free to go on hating the cause of my misfortune, but to never think of the world as an evil place. I may hate the Noble that took my sight, but I must not blame any of the others. The Nobility are alive as we are, and as long as they exist, they stray and suffer as we do. That is why I do not hate the Nobility." Raking up her loose hairs, Leticia urged him. "Now compose a song for me, please."

Then came Greylancer's astounding answer: "You have been warned—it will be poorly composed."

"Yes, all right." The golden-haired girl nodded once, her dress looking like the most becoming garment in all the world.

The girl closed her eyes and stood beneath the blue sky.

Were Greylancer to reveal that he'd composed a song before, the Nobles might fold up in laughter at the world's greatest joke ever told.

Yet, in fact, he had.

Just one verse.

Greylancer searched for it in the cobwebs of memory.

After the wind stroked his hair a second time, out of his crimson lips came a song:

When first you entered with a shadow and began to dance
I could not see the controlling strings
Dance, will you
Dance, will you
Cut the strings of fate into the night and dance
And make Fate fall in step with me

Waves of grass nodded their approbation. The wind blew. Twilight wrapped the nightsong and its poet in an embrace.

CHAPTER 5:
THE ARCHER
NAMED ARROW

1

When his voice faded, Leticia stared at the grasslands in the distance. Despite the darkness of the song, she appeared bathed in light. "That's the first song I heard other than my mother's."

"Do you like it?"

"Oh, very much," she said, squeezing her hands in front of her chest. "But it's a sad song."

"Sad?" Greylancer felt a peculiar feeling come over him. The word he'd uttered was an emotion he'd not recalled feeling before.

From whence had this emotion been borne?

And what had brought it on?

He felt his consciousness drift terribly far away...

And then a door flew open.

A glittering chandelier. Men and women dressed in evening attire. A party? But when? Then—

His consciousness weaved and slipped deftly between the night dwellers and emerged onto the veranda, where the marble floor reflected the moonlight.

She stood in the crowd of partygoers milling about like shadows.

Perhaps the white dress had been spun from moonlight. Her face was obscured from view, as her bare shoulders and back shimmered like water.

Call out her name, Greylancer.

He closed his eyes. He was at a ball.

Yes, her name—

Slowly, the woman began to turn around.

Her name escapes me, but if I glimpse her face—

The distant sound of wheels rumbled from the depths of night.

†

The Noble's eyes fluttered open.

Greylancer shot a hard look in the direction of the sound, but he could make out nothing more than waves of grass.

"Is something wrong?" Leticia asked, sensing a change in her companion.

"A wagon approaches."

After straining her ears toward the road, the girl said, "I don't hear anything."

A Noble's ears were capable of picking up noises several kilometers away. "Your companion comes this way."

"Huh?"

"Too late."

"What?"

"Something else is coming this way. It must have sniffed out the smell of blood. Do you know your way back to the road?"

"Yes."

"Keep low and run."

"What is—"

"A monster. It's coming straight at us from the west. Quickly."

"What about you?"

"I'll manage. You should know I am immortal."

"You're talking like a Noble. Come, we'll run together."

Greylancer looked at the girl's desperate face and then down at his lower body.

If the girl were somehow persuaded to reattach his body, he would regain his freedom in an instant.

"Go!" he barked. The sound of a Noble's roar.

†

"Now what?" muttered Greylancer.

He did not appear to be in a terrible panic. A Noble would rise again even after being devoured by a monster. But being torn to pieces without a fight was something his pride would not allow.

"Move." He threw his consciousness into his right hand. "Move, damn it. Move!"

Something bright and colorful thrashed through the grass and appeared before him.

The stout, one-meter body and eight legs stretching ten meters were yellow with black speckles.

Its shape was similar to that of a giant spider. It halted its advance and eyed Greylancer.

"A ghost spider. Damn that Mayerling. Allowing these behemoths to run loose. And he calls himself a human sympathizer."

The surface of the spherical body that could be called neither the cephalothorax nor abdomen split open in the shape of a cross and a face appeared out of the opening.

It was the face of a middle-aged man.

"The last victim." Greylancer twisted his lips in amusement. Feeding exclusively on humans, the monster was also called a *human-faced spider* because it reproduced the face of the last prey it devoured.

More spiders appeared on either side of the first: one with the face of a white-haired old woman and the other with the face of a boy of sixteen or seventeen. The living faces of the humans emanated a ghastly aura.

"I've tired of lying here. Come and get me." The words were spoken in provocation. After eying Greylancer suspiciously, the human faces slackened and broke into eerie smiles.

The three arachnids quickly closed the five-meter distance.

The face of the middle-aged man opened its enormous mouth to bite off Greylancer's head, when something rained down from above.

From where had they been shot?

How had the bowman taken aim? What was but a blur tracing a beautiful arc downward transformed into three scarlet arrows and skewered the spiders from the back to front.

The spiders let out a hideous scream. Because of their screams and blood that poisoned the area, the prairie withered afterward and would never grow another blade of grass within a two-kilometer radius.

"Well now." While the three spiders writhed in the throes of death, Greylancer admired the dexterity of the archer lurking somewhere in the grass.

Based on the angles of entry, the archer figured to be over two hundred meters away. Sighting the spiders from that distance hardly seemed possible. Was it possible, then, to hit a target without seeing it? Three of them, no less?

The spiders fell sideways at Greylancer's feet.

At the same time, the human faces stole out of captivity, leaving a hole in the quivering bodies.

Eight legs sprouted out of each of the faces and carried them into the tall grass in the blink of an eye.

As soon as they disappeared, the creaking of a wagon drew closer. Within a minute, a wagon drawn by a headless cybernetic horse emerged from the road.

Next to the young man holding the reins and bow sat Leticia.

The boy jumped off the wagon and ran toward Greylancer, notching an arrow in his bow.

But his feet carried him no further than five steps. *He* was not blind.

The moment he mouthed the word, "Noble," his consciousness was taken from him. Greylancer's eyes burned red.

"Come," the Greater Noble said.

The youth, bow still pulled ready, began to walk with slow, unsteady steps. Even as his will was taken from him, his subconscious was fighting tooth and nail to resist.

When he finally stood next to where Greylancer lay, the Noble commanded, "Bring my lower half and attach it."

The well-dressed young man must come from Leticia's adoptive family. Probably an older brother, given his rugged looks, and how he'd come to fetch Leticia. Above all, he was the human to whom Greylancer owed his life.

The Greater Noble paid no mind to such trifles. He was an overlord, and aside from supplying him periodically with blood, the human boy was a worthless barnyard animal under his protection.

Easing the tension in the bow, the boy rested the weapon by his feet.

His awkward movements suggested the ongoing battle for his will.

When Greylancer touched his legs at last, he smiled a satisfied smile.

The boy had managed to carry out the frightful task.

Sweat dripped from his brow. It was more the result of the struggle between his mind and will than of physical labor.

"That will do." Greylancer nodded, his eyes glowing blood red. "Tell me your name."

"Arrow Belsen," answered the boy, mortified. Greylancer's smile grew wider. "How can...a Noble...in broad daylight...?" he gasped, his spirit not yet broken.

Greylancer ignored him and asked, "How old are you?"

"Twenty."

"Such ruddy cheeks...how warm and sweet the blood flowing through that body must be." Greylancer was able to raise his right arm. The dormant power began to reawaken in his now whole body. "Come here."

The right hand beckoned.

The youth resisted as sweat dripped from his chin and dissolved into the dirt.

His body bucked and bowed several times, until finally he was brought to his knees before the Greater Noble.

"Petty human." Greylancer grabbed the boy's black hair and

wrenched his neck toward his chest so the carotid artery came before his eyes. "Well now." The vampire's red lips opened before the rapidly ending day.

"Arrow?" The girl's voice forced Greylancer to pull away. When he spotted Leticia approaching with the aid of her stick, his sinister intentions were shaken. Perhaps with the instinct of the blind, she came to a halt just short of the two men. "I can sense the two of you about here. Arrow, are you there?"

"Yeah." The boy pulled away from Greylancer and stood up. Snatching the bow up off the ground, he returned the arrow to the quiver on his back. "I went through an ungodly experience, but it's over now."

"I'm glad. Thank you."

"There are three dead ghost spiders here. Don't come any closer."

"You killed them, didn't you? You're so brave."

"It's nothing." Arrow looked down at Greylancer and asked, "Can you walk?"

"I'll manage." Greylancer shot a glance at Leticia. "Is he your true love?"

"That's right." It was Arrow that answered. Leticia could only blush and nod.

"He is a good man. I wish you a happy life."

"Thank you."

"We should go back to the wagon. It will be dark soon," said Arrow. "He can stay the night with us."

"That's a wonderful idea." Leticia smiled, suspecting nothing of the true nature of her current circumstance. "This man is a troubadour," she informed Arrow, as they walked together back to the wagon.

Watching protectively over her every step, Arrow nodded. "Oh, so he's a bard."

"He even composed a lovely song for me. I wish you could have heard it."

"Not a chance."

"Arrow!" Leticia admonished. "I'm sorry, he's always this way."

"So you are his adopted sister," said Greylancer, walking several paces in front of the couple.

"That's right," Arrow answered again. "But we want to be together."

"That sounds fine."

"When that day comes, would you come to our wedding?"

Arrow's eyes grew wide at Leticia's request. "Now wait a minute, this man is—"

"A troubadour," said Leticia, "with lovely songs to sing. Would you write a song like the one earlier for our wedding? I promise to send you an invitation."

"If your invitation should ever find me."

"Oh," Leticia gasped. She began again, sounding as if she might cry, "What shall I do? How will we keep in touch? I know, you can write to me! Not every day, or once a week. Once a month. And if you'll tell me where you are and where you're going next…" Her face clouded again. "No…that won't do. A troubadour travels daily. Perhaps you should write me once a week. If you don't mind."

Greylancer didn't know why. Perhaps it was the way she had tacked on, "If you don't mind." Whatever the reason, the Noble let out a full-throated laugh. "Very well. Once a week then. If you so desire to hear my song."

"Yes, I do."

"Listen to you," Arrow muttered sullenly. "So much more cheerful now."

2

The three climbed onto the wagon.

After the cybernetic horse started into a gallop, Greylancer asked, "Who taught you the bow?"

"A traveling bowman." Arrow cracked the whip, and the horse accelerated.

"The wicked bow skill—the ability to fell an unsighted target. Fewer than ten Nobles are known to practice it. What is your range?"

"The farthest I've attempted is two kilometers. But my master succeeded from over ten kilometers."

"How is it you accomplish this?"

"I can hit any target I've seen once, whether he's inside a house, underground in a wine cellar, or on a moving boat. I don't need to see him firsthand. I can look at a picture or drawing."

"What if you can do neither?"

"I can listen to a detailed description and shoot."

"And when you're unable to do that?"

"If I had a strand of the target's hair, a sliver of skin, a part of a nail…"

"Nothing of the kind."

"Then I'd have to go by the name alone."

"Hm, can you do it?"

"But the accuracy goes down to ten percent."

"A formidable skill." It was a sincere appraisal. That the boy was human did nothing to lower the Noble's estimation of his skill. Such was the measure of the Noble named Greylancer. Then, he asked a frightful question: "Have you ever felled a Noble?"

"Alas, no. My master hasn't either. But if I had a mind to, I wouldn't miss."

The wagon rattled down the road in silence for nearly an hour before entering the tiny village.

Arrow and Leticia's house stood just west of the village square.

The farmhouse was spacious and made of lavish materials, as might be expected of a family affluent enough to adopt.

The three climbed down from the wagon inside the barn.

"I'll be by with a blanket later," said Arrow.

"Arrow, what are you saying?" Leticia said. "We can't have a guest sleep in the barn!"

"It's all right," said Greylancer. "Your brother knows well how to treat me. It is the proper way."

Hearing this, Leticia could say nothing more. "What will

Mother and Father say?"

"I'll explain to them later." With this curt response, Arrow left the barn.

"My brother is acting very strangely," said Leticia, to which Greylancer answered, "He is only doing what I requested."

"When was that?"

"In the grasslands, before you returned."

"Why won't you come inside the house?"

"We troubadours are not easy around others. It's far easier to be alone with our words."

Each utterance weighed heavily like iron. Leticia nodded in satisfaction. "Then I'll be back later to bring you dinner. I hope you can tell me about all the places you've seen then."

Then Leticia padded out of the barn.

Beneath the sixty-watt light bulb, Greylancer stood alone. Around him were haystacks, hoes, spades, and scythes of various sizes, a wooden cart, sacks of fertilizer and seeds, along with the sprayers to disperse them. They took up space in the century-old barn as if they had been waiting for Greylancer for as long.

It was a strangely familiar scene, the reason for which Greylancer already realized.

"Was her name...Michia?" The village chief's wife, whom Greylancer had cut down with his lance. He had watched her die in a barn much like this one. "The night is still young. There is no telling what will happen. But first, a proper feast."

His cape swelled like the ocean. It was the wind.

Like an actor walking onto a stage before an audience, Greylancer strode out of the open door and into the night.

†

As soon as Leticia returned to the main house, the family took their seats at the dinner table.

Leticia began by regaling them with the tale of the troubadour who'd sung her a song.

"Why that's wonderful," said her mother. Her plump face broke into a broad smile. "I don't know about troubadours, but he sounds like a generous man. He makes his living from singing."

"Then again, I imagine most men would do anything for my Leticia," said her father, who was surprisingly skinny for a farm owner. A blind girl was an impractical presence on a farm. Nevertheless the kindly farmer had said, "A pretty girl like Leticia? Why her presence alone would brighten up our lives," and brought her into the family. From that day forward, the girl had never forgotten her gratitude.

True to his words, Leticia's adoptive parents accepted her like their own. Only Arrow remained gruff with her, but in time, she realized that his outward demeanor belied his kind heart.

The maid Miranda and manservant Alts looked after her.

They spoke little, but both helpers attended to their duties and did not once treat Leticia cruelly because she was adopted.

But it was Miranda, setting out the bowls of stew she'd ladled from a large pot before the others, who remarked, "This bard seems a bit rude, if you ask me. Here he's been taken into a stranger's home, albeit the barn, and he doesn't even bother to say thanks. It's ungentlemanly, eh, Alts?"

The stoutly built manservant was in the dining room fixing the broken fireplace.

He did not answer right away, but once he'd finished the repairs, he asked in a flat voice, "You sure he's really a troubadour?" adding, "I saw one years ago in the Eastern Frontier. I'd expected a troubadour to be stately in bearing and appearance… turned out to be this dirty old vagabond with a banged-up lyre. Didn't even look at the children hanging on him to sing them a song. I heard he was taken in by the village chief and ended up writing a good ten, twenty pieces in exchange for meals and lodging. Two or three years later, one of the verses he'd composed on that night had gotten out, and—it was as awful as if I'd written it. Even a newborn child could have sung it. That's what everyone thought at the time. But it's not about the song," Alts said, casting a sideways glance at the girl. "My point is, Miss Leticia, troubadours are stingy that way. That's what it takes to survive."

"Are you saying this troubadour is a fake?" Miranda narrowed her eyes.

"I don't know. Just that no one would be so generous with the art that feeds him."

"Arrow?" The father shot a glance at the boy silently working his spoon into the stew.

"I can't say whether he's a troubadour or not, but he's definitely not a man."

"What was that?"

"I meant that he's…not a *bad* man."

"I agree," Leticia chimed in. "The song he composed was sad and very lovely. Sure, he frightened me a little at first, but he's very kind."

Leticia's parents looked at each other. They recognized that their daughter's appraisal was far more accurate than that of the sighted.

"If Leticia says so, he must be," said her father, to which Miranda shrugged in half-hearted protest, and there was no more talk about the bard in the barn.

"By the way, Arrow. You're not still thinking about joining the Nobility's army, are you?" the mother asked, tearing a bite out of a roll so hard it made her lips curl.

The boy's answer was enough to make a mother cry. "It's not the army. It's the guard corps, in charge of guarding Noble graves during the day."

"Why would a human do something so horrible?"

"Because only humans can do it."

"But I thought they have machines for that."

"The OSB's technology is more advanced. Who's to say the OSB won't sabotage the mechanized guards to turn against their masters? No, humans make the ideal guards. Not to mention the status of standing by the Nobles' side, not as a servant but as their protector."

"That may be, but why you…"

After the mother's words trailed away, the father asked bluntly, "Think of the danger you'd be putting us in. What if the Anti-Nobility Alliance comes after us?"

"No problem. I'll just tell them that you have to jump into the bosom of the enemy to strike them down. The Alliance is so blind with rage that they'll send me off into the lion's lair with tears of joy in their eyes."

"Even so—"

"To be honest, I'm not all that interested in the Nobility or humans, for that matter. All I want to know is whether the Nobility will recognize the wicked bow skills that Master Slade passed on to me."

"What the Nobility need now are not archers but telepaths, I've heard."

"If it doesn't work out, fine. But I'm not going to be able to live with myself without at least trying."

Mother and father looked at each other, sighed and returned to their meal. Only Leticia silently applauded his determination. She adored her taciturn and courageous brother, who liked to make silly jokes when they were alone.

†

After dinner, as Leticia got up to deliver a bowl of stew to Greylancer, there was a visit from Savagonin and his wife from next door.

After apologizing for their abrupt visit, Savagonin began, "We saw this giant of a man on our way to see the village chief. I think it was a Noble." His voice trembled. His wife wrapped her scarf tighter around her neck.

"It can't be," the father said forthrightly. "The overseer forbids unannounced visits. No one would dare disobey him."

Cinching up his scarf, Savagonin added, "You know, he looked exactly like the overseer of the Northern Frontier. No, I'm certain it's him."

"The overseer of the North is Lord Greylancer. I don't believe it. What would he be doing here?"

"I haven't a clue," Savagonin's wife said, her voice strained. "But that ominous, imposing figure. That cape. He had to be a Noble…and one of some importance, I know it." Her bloodshot eyes turned to Arrow. "You're handy with a bow. Would you track him down and find out what he's doing here? We can take you to the place where we saw him. That's what we came here to ask."

Leticia could feel her heart about to burst. An imposing figure wearing a cape. Could it be…?

"All right, I'll get my bow." Arrow rose from his chair.

"Now wait a minute, Arrow," said his mother. "Why must you—"

"Don't worry. I'll recruit some help on the way," Arrow said coolly and exited.

His father said nothing, resigned to the daily reality of living in the Frontier ruled by the Nobility.

3

Arrow went to his room where he slung his quiver over his shoulder and grabbed his bow before going to the barn to confirm the bard's absence. The answer was evident soon enough.

Letica appeared behind him. "Mr. No-Name. He isn't here, is he?"

"No."

"He can't be a Noble, can he? It was light out when we met him."

"Right."

"Then the Noble that Mr. and Mrs. Savagonin saw couldn't have been Mr. No-Name."

"No, it had to be."

Leticia stared at her betrothed in astonishment. "What do you mean?"

"You've heard the stories—about the Noble who walks under

the sun." Arrow began to pace and brushed past Leticia.

"Of course I have. But those are just stories."

"Not necessarily. I heard from the Anti-Nobility Alliance that the Sacred Ancestor has the Science Center in the Capital working on a number of projects. One of them is called the Vampires Living in the Day Project."

"What a long name."

"Long is right." Arrow's voice came from behind Leticia.

"But that's not possible. A Noble walking about during the day. I don't believe it."

"Believe it." Arrow wrapped his arms around her neck.

"No." Try as she might, she could not wriggle free. Feeling his hot breath on the nape of her neck, Leticia let out an imperceptible moan. "We mustn't—not here."

"We'll be married soon enough." He brought his lips to her pale flesh, making Leticia gasp. Pulling away immediately, he said, "So the bard is a Noble...but if you ask me, there are others who are more suspicious."

"Who?"

"What happened to the Savagonins?"

"They left while you were in your room. You don't think..."

"Did you notice how they both kept fixing their scarves? Maybe they did more than see the Noble."

"Do you mean they were bitten?"

"I'm afraid not," said a calm voice.

Arrow and Leticia twirled around in the direction of the voice. "Mr. and Mrs. Savagonin?"

Unlike earlier, the couple stood in the barn, smiling. "We haven't been bitten. Look!" Mrs. Savagonin pulled down her scarf. Her neck was tinted yellow with black speckles.

"It's true we encountered the Noble," said Savagonin. "We were about to feast on him in the prairie, but you got in the way. We came here to express our gratitude—but after feeding on this couple first." He unfurled his scarf, revealing his brightly colored neck.

Long nails grew out of the man's fingers, each of the digits sprouting into gangling legs and feelers before Arrow's and Leticia's very eyes.

"The ghost spiders." No sooner had Arrow said it than the impostors' clothes were torn away. "There were three of you. Where is the third?"

"Paying a visit to your parents." The woman's voice descended from three meters above. Attached to its neck was a squat, ovular body, held up by eight legs measuring ten meters.

"Tsk, two siblings carrying out a secret affair. Where is your bow now? Whoa—too late!" The male spider's legs lashed out, sending the bow flying across the barn and crashing against the far wall. "We'll make short work of the Noble when he returns. He's probably out drinking his fill of human blood. It must be quite a feast."

"Exactly right."

The spiders recoiled in shock. When they shot a look at the entrance, the wind let out a sharp whistle.

The spider with the face of the female Savagonin was lifted up and suspended five meters in the air.

Greylancer stood entranced by the silver lance impaling the spider, its face already frozen in the throes of death, as blood gushed like a waterfall down the handle. "I discerned your true identity just as you did mine. A sense of foreboding brought me back here soon after sating my thirst, and lo and behold, here you are. Pity—if you'd not harbored thoughts of revenge, perhaps you might have lived a day longer. Look at how you writhe and suffer. Vermin that you are, nothing is more precious than the pleasure of watching a woman meet her end."

The nameless troubadour pulled back the lance and struck again.

The female spider's body flew off the lance, crashed against the ceiling, and exploded into pieces.

Greylancer spun around and looked overhead.

The male spider—Savagonin had jumped and now clung to the ceiling.

Moonlight poured in from the one-meter square skylight

above. Savagonin broke through the window headfirst and slipped out, stretching his eight legs behind him like an octopus.

As shards of glass rained down around him like jewels, Greylancer kicked the ground. Grabbing the window frame with one hand, he hoisted himself up onto the roof in one motion. Barely looking around, he spotted Savagonin scurrying away and leaping onto the next roof.

It was the very silhouette of a giant spider leaping beneath the moonlight.

"Arrow," Greylancer called down below. "Can you shoot him down? Do not disgrace your master's name."

The answer was a sharp, whizzing noise from the window. Only Greylancer's eyes were able to recognize the arrow.

The fiendish instincts of the spider, already but a speck in the distance, sensed its coming.

The spider jumped from the roof. The house was located at the end of the road, across from which was a square, where there stood the gutted remains of a religious building and a stone hut made of three enormous slabs.

Fifty years ago, a research team sent from the Capital had discovered a sarcophagus enshrined underground. Contained within the sarcophagus was a mummified humanoid creature dating back three thousand years; its origin was never identified. Though the research team had taken with them its garments, necklaces, and various other articles, the results of the analysis were never made known to the village.

The ghost spider slipped inside the hut. It was completely enclosed in stone, so not even a razor blade could enter the chamber. The spider's was the only route in and out of the hut. There was no way an arrow shot from the rear could enter.

The spider allowed himself a moment's peace. It was still smarting from the pain and terror of when its parent body was shot down in the prairie. One of its three lungs let out a breath.

Then the ghost spider expelled what breath was left in its remaining lungs.

Before the spider realized the arrow had entered through the front and pierced a hole in the middle of its forehead clear through the back, the spider was already dead.

†

"Got him?" Greylancer asked, after jumping from the roof and landing next to Arrow in the barn.

Arrow nodded and grunted his satisfaction at having proved his skill, following his three kills from earlier in the day.

"There is another. Go."

"All right." Notching another arrow in the bow, Arrow ran for the main house.

Drawing a bead on wherever the target might be, stopping at nothing to shoot through its jugular—such was the meaning of the wicked bow's existence.

The proud, even arrogant expression on the Noble's face vanished instantly like light snow upon looking at the lithe shadow. "Leticia."

The girl, who adored the nameless troubadour, shook her pretty head. "Who was it that sang that song for me?"

"It was I," Greylancer answered.

"Who are you?"

"Greylancer—overseer of the Northern Frontier sector."

"Then I do not know you." Leticia's voice sounded exceedingly mournful and clear at the same time. "The man who gave me my song was someone who traveled distant lands. Someone who'd promised to tell me about all the things he'd witnessed and seen. Someone who'd bashfully composed a very lovely and sad song. Why didn't you feed on my blood?"

"I must take my leave." Greylancer set out toward the wagon. A siren blared from the open door. The emergency alarm. "Someone must have discovered my blood victim. I commend the rest to you."

"Is that why...you came?"

"I couldn't bring myself to drink your blood. Your brother

has only been hypnotized. I will release him when I've left the village. I wish you a happy life."

The giant exited through the barn door and returned pulling a cybernetic horse. After hitching it to the wagon, he climbed on and said, "Fare thee well."

The girl pointed a pale finger outside. "You should go to the West Country Highway and head north by northeast."

After a breath, Greylancer said, "You have my gratitude," and flicked the reins.

The wagon sped off out of the barn.

Leticia stood there until the rattling of the wagon left the property and receded into the night.

Dance, will you

Dance, will you

Cut the strings of fate into the night

Several minutes later, Arrow returned and informed Leticia that he had avenged the death of their parents, who'd been killed by the elusive third ghost spider.

CHAPTER 6:
THE BENEVOLENT
OVERLORD

1

Greylancer had scarcely driven an hour out of the village when a gyrocopter appeared in the sky.

A floodlight shone down upon the wagon on the highway and its driver. Greylancer did not halt the wagon as the light chased after from behind.

"We are with the patrol force under Lord Mayerling's command," said a voice issuing forth from the gyrocopter. "Excuse me, but you bear the appearance of a Noble. Please state your name and destination."

"The name is Greylancer. My destination—"

"Yes, I thought it might be you," the voice of the patrolman interrupted. "My ignorance notwithstanding, please forgive my impudence. Allow me to escort you to the overseer's castle."

"No!"

"Pardon?"

"I intend to return directly to my dominion. Tell the others I want no more interruptions during my journey."

"That would make me delinquent in my duties." The voice of the patrolman sounded rattled. "The reports of your disappearance came directly from the OSB attack force, and the Capital has issued a search order throughout the world including the Frontier. It is an honor to find you here in this territory, of all places. Please come with us, I beseech you."

"What is my name?" The Noble's voice that seemed to spout from the earth shook the gyrocopter.

"Lord Greylancer."

"I will not go, I tell you."

The voice from the gyrocopter fell silent. After the wagon began to creep ahead of the floodlight, the patrolman said, "But…"

"If you require an excuse, tell Mayerling that I find him disagreeable."

The wagon continued on its way.

Five minutes later, a massive gyrodyne appeared before Greylancer.

This aircraft exceeded one hundred meters in length and bristled with military accoutrements reminiscent of lances and swords. It was plain for anyone to see that this aircraft belonged to a Noble, no less one from a long line of war hawks.

"What is a warrior the likes of Greylancer doing riding such a rickety box?" said a booming voice.

Peering up, Greylancer said scornfully, "Zeus Macula…" and continued to drive the wagon.

"Wait, wait. As surly as ever, I see. I knew you would turn up alive somewhere. Well now, perhaps the fates have conspired for us to meet. I've been visiting with the invertebrate…er, I mean Mayerling. What say we renew old friendships?"

"Reprehensible!"

Zeus let out a full-throated laugh. "Yes, yes. I expected as much. I didn't imagine you'd get along with the boy."

"Or with you."

Zeus was silent, and then, "All right, all right. But surely the Northern overlord cannot leave the West without paying respect to its ruler. Besides which, you'll be interested to know the Privy Council has made several decisions during your absence. With that wagon your return to the North will take three nights. Perhaps you'd care to know sooner."

The wagon stopped.

Three minutes later, Greylancer and Zeus were drinking from red glasses in the Western Frontier sector overlord's sitting room.

"What is this swill? Hardly anything to serve a guest." Zeus slammed his glass on the table and began to pace the room with long strides.

"Synthetic blood." Greylancer drained his drink and stared at the glass, the crystal cup sparkling a different hue of red than the drink it once contained. "If the overlord drinks it, then his vassals can only do likewise. The humans are spared from having to pay blood tribute, which is why, far from being hated, Mayerling is extolled as a compassionate ruler."

"He's merely playing the hero. Nothing more than a young buck ingratiating himself to the humans and reveling in his own reputation as a benevolent dictator."

"Point that finger somewhere else," Greylancer said.

The Eastern overlord lowered his right arm. "Pardon me." As injured as Zeus sounded, he gave away no hint of anger. His rival was simply too formidable.

Anyone knowing Greylancer well would say that he was the image of equanimity. Zeus had informed him that the attack on the OSB moon base had succeeded; the surviving OSB fled to Mars. Not only had the battle ended with fewer than ten Nobility casualties, Greylancer's corps had returned unscathed.

Zeus held back from revealing the Privy Council's decision until Mayerling joined them.

"What are you plotting?" Greylancer arched a brow.

"Nothing at all," protested Zeus, but his entire being seemed to conceal a hundred machinations. The ruler of the Eastern Frontier sector was a man born for chicanery. "Now don't besmirch my good name. Why must you think such things of me?"

"Because you've brought me here. Knowing you, I would have expected you to send me on my way and then fire a missile at my back."

"Now, now, I'm wounded that you see me in such a light, my friend."

"You misunderstand the concept of friendship."

"Now, now."

"I told you to point that finger somewhere else."

Zeus did not yield this time.

Realizing the Noble was not pointing at him, Greylancer turned around.

A figure shrouded in a purple cape stood at the door, which had opened unnoticed.

A youthful, handsome face curved the same red lips as the others into a smile.

This was Lord Mayerling, overseer of the Western Frontier sector. "Welcome, my lords," he said, dispensing with calling them by name. He approached the others, and noting the glasses on the table, he said, "The drink doesn't agree with you, I see. No matter, you can well savor the sweet stuff in your respective sectors. Lord Zeus Macula, forgive me for keeping you waiting."

"Not at all, Lord Greylancer here has been a welcome distraction. Going out to collect him helped pass the time." As magnanimous as he sounded, the words were dripping with sarcasm.

Unruffled, Mayerling began, "I've had a look at the Privy Council's missive. So tell me what brought you here."

"Then I'll leave you two to your business," said Greylancer, turning on his heels.

"Wait, wait," said Zeus. "You must hear me out. I've already notified the North of my intention to visit. This fortuitous gathering couldn't be more convenient. A godsend, really."

"Let's have it," Mayerling said.

"The Privy Council was greatly pleased by the victory on the OSB moon base and has declared the day a worldwide day of celebration," began Zeus. "A matter of common knowledge to all save one."

The *one* sipped the synthetic blood after pouring himself another glass from the gold carafe.

"The Privy Council has come to another decision, per-haps buoyed by their latest victory and the imminent day of reckoning," Zeus continued. "In four days' time, on the Sacred Ancestor's birthday, they have decided to wipe out the OSB vanguard lurking all across this world."

Mayerling looked back at Zeus in shock, while Greylancer stopped the glass at his lips.

"Why were we not informed?" asked Mayerling, fighting back anger. He need not question the veracity of the information. Zeus Macula's information was known to be infallible. There were rumors that Zeus was a bastard child of a member of the Privy Council.

"How do they propose to do it?" Greylancer asked, the glass frozen in his hand.

"Their plan is to carry out a plasma attack on the locations where OSB infiltrators are believed to be hiding. Plasma weapons are only fatal to the OSB and local human populations. I suspect the decree will be handed down tomorrow or the day after."

"That's absurd!" roared Mayerling.

"I assume your outrage is directed at the Privy Council who chose to slight us." After shooting an icy look at the young Noble, Zeus looked meaningfully at Greylancer and at Mayerling again. "Of course, this is hardly the first time the Capital has decided to disregard the Frontier. The Privy Council thinks of us as a bunch of country Nobles who've fallen from the Capital's good graces. This sentiment is also what begat this slight. But let us not forget, since the Capital and Frontier were established we overseers have been accorded complete control over the Frontier."

Zeus Macula was referring to what was called *absolute managerial rights*.

As long as each of the sectors supplied the Capital with the blood tribute it demanded, the overseers were given complete administrative control over the Frontier's political and economic affairs. Furthermore, it was the overseers that carried out the Capital's orders, but whether such orders were carried out or not depended entirely on the overseers' consent or refusal. In a way, this tolerant, albeit lax system reflected the magnanimity of the

Privy Council but was also influenced by the immortality of the Noble race. As long as those in the Capital were kept sufficiently sated with blood, thereby relieving them of worries, they did not concern themselves with trivial matters.

In this case, the human population was a trivial matter.

We will allow you full reign over the Frontier so long as you do not interfere with the Capital's decisions. This implicit agreement simply did not pass muster with the three overseers.

Nobles that they were, vampires valued pride above everything else. However, the rigor with which the overseers sought to preserve it in the Frontier vastly differed from the vampires residing in the Capital. No, that chasm between the Privy Council and the overseer was one surpassing the realm of tragedy, verging on the comedic.

"Given their disregard for our managerial rights, we must take measures to make the Privy Council acknowledge their wrongdoing. Any objections?"

The handsome young Noble cast an icy look at Zeus's fevered face. "How do you plan to do it?"

"Answer me first. Do you have any objections?"

"What say Mircalla in the South?"

"The female persuasion can be tricky. I thought to discuss it with you first."

"I believe I was an afterthought," Greylancer said casually

Zeus's expression tensed. "Well, now…" he said, an audible smile in his voice. He grimaced and continued, "My seeing you here is a fortunate coincidence, to be sure. But my intention has always been to seek the approval of the overseers."

"Whichever the case, I intend to go to the Capital before raising any objections," Mayerling declared. "I refuse to overlook such an act of barbarism. I shall roundly denounce the members of the Privy Council myself."

2

"Now don't go off half-cocked." Zeus held up both hands with an air of reluctance and smiled bitterly, knowing well the young Noble's impetuousness. "If you do that, we will all be removed from power. You will be putting all of us in the crossfire."

"I don't give a damn about the rest of you! See if they dare use their plasma cannons against my people. On my life and family name, I shall put a stop to this madness!" Mayerling said, seething.

"And what then?" countered Greylancer. Mayerling froze. "If you resign your post, another Noble will take your place. Do you think he will rule over your people as you have?"

The young Noble could say nothing.

"Greylancer is right," said Zeus. "Your benevolent rule over the humans will come to naught. Let me handle the Privy Council."

"After they've fired their plasma cannons?"

Zeus turned toward Greylancer, aghast as if he'd read his mind. Taking no more than a second to hide his shock, he asked brazenly, "What ever do you mean, Greylancer?"

"No meaning at all. Merely stating a foregone conclusion. The Zeus Macula I know would do exactly as I stated."

"Yes." Zeus nodded emphatically. "That is exactly my plan. If I persuaded them to suspend their attack and succeeded, I would only become beholden to the Privy Council, and that would be—"

"Meaningless?" Greylancer's eyes emitted a certain light that seemed to see through Zeus's eyes.

"Just what do you plan to do after the plasma attack?" said Mayerling, stepping forward. His anger had killed any expression on his face. Only his scarlet lips burned in his pale white visage.

He stopped about five paces short of where Zeus stood. A Noble lacking self-control would never be entrusted with overseeing the Frontier.

With an unflinching gaze, Zeus answered, "To bring official

charges against the Privy Council for violating our absolute managerial rights and for the indiscriminate slaughter of its subjects. To purge the Privy Council of its current members and to create a new decision-making body."

"With you as its head, no doubt," said Mayerling quietly.

"Exactly right. And what of it?" Zeus thrust out his chest, both Mayerling and Greylancer nearly dimmed by his dignified air. "Have you ever pondered the notion of immortality?" Zeus circled the room and took up a position where he could regard both men. "This very nature that has promised the Nobility eternal prosperity has now become our greatest enemy. You must have sensed it for yourselves every time you entered the Capital, sensed the unspeakable malaise the entire city—from the Privy Council to the research facilities and affiliate organizations—has been mired in.

"It is an inevitable outcome of immortality. Our scientific progress to grant us our physical wants has also contributed to this. Eternal fulfillment—is this not what every intelligent being covets? Surely, there exist more evolved beings than the Nobility. Could more civilizations exist in the distant stars? Could our science achieve greater discoveries? Such questions were the foundation of progress. But time has passed since the rulers in the Capital have showed any interest or appreciation for such pursuits. Our civilization has come to full maturity. You see that, don't you? We have run against the limits of eternal life. It is an unspeakable tragedy. It is my opinion that the OSB invasion has done more to help us regain our fervor to live than anything else. With weapons in hand, we have plunged into battle once more. Our blood boils again. Who but we will break through the limits of the Nobility world and open our people to new possibilities?" With a wave of a hand, Zeus Macula concluded his speech, spellbound by his own rhetoric.

"Quite an impassioned speech." It was Greylancer who answered. "But surely, you cannot believe the Privy Council will agree to a forced retirement?"

"That would take a miracle." Zeus smiled. "As soon as I bring charges against them, the Privy Council will use the full extent of their authority and might to oust us. But not to worry; I have already taken necessary measures. There are those in the Capital who are willing to fall in line behind me. They number about a hundred."

"Only a hundred?" cried Mayerling in disbelief. "Sheer madness, I tell you! I shall cast my lot with the Privy Council."

"Only a fool general who has never commanded an army would think a hundred too few, Mayerling. How many men do you think it would take to sabotage the Capital's antiproton reactor? It only takes one. We have a hundred. How many would dare stand against us? A hundred? No, I count fewer than ten. Once the Capital lies in ashes, disposing of them will be an easy task."

"We haven't yet destroyed the OSB," Mayerling spat viciously. "They're lurking somewhere in space, watching and waiting for just the right moment to conquer this planet. And you are dreaming of a revolution?"

"The OSB will require some time to regroup. The damage that Greylancer wrought upon their operations was considerable. The Privy Council will be caught sleeping. Now is our time to rise up and unseat them. Join me, Greylancer, Mayerling. Take my hand." Looking upon the two men with unflinching resolve, Zeus held out his muscular hands.

"I will not," Mayerling said flatly. "I will proceed as planned. This genocide must not be allowed to happen."

"I expected as much from the benevolent overlord. You and I will discuss it further. And now, what say you, Greylancer?"

"If we can eradicate the OSB's advance guard, we will have to bear some sacrifice. They're humans—they hardly count as a sacrifice."

Zeus twisted his lips into a grin, while Mayerling closed his eyes. "Excellent."

Ignoring the overseer stepping forward with a proffered hand, Greylancer said, "But I will be party to neither side. Mayerling, you head for the Capital at once. Zeus, I suppose you will have to discuss matters with Mircalla. I shall return north."

"Very well." Clenching his outstretched hand into a fist, Zeus Macula moved toward the table, snatched the carafe, and gulped down the drink in a matter of seconds. "The fact that you have concocted this blood substitute is evidence enough of your impotence. I refuse to spend a second more in such odious company. I'll show myself out. Farewell, Greylancer." Zeus turned and stalked out, leaving only the high echo of footsteps behind him.

"What now?" Greylancer asked the young overseer.

"There isn't a moment to lose. I must depart for the Capital immediately. I will have my retainers see you back to your sector."

"That won't be necessary. But I could do with a change of wagon." Greylancer seemed to be frowning. Whether he was thinking about the plasma storm that would devastate the land or struggling to devise a strategy against the OSB, his expression resembled that of anguish.

†

Mayerling's mansion appeared much like the old-world castles of other Nobles, but the buildings scattered beneath the moonlight were as elegant as one might expect of the young Noble.

Upon being escorted by a silver-haired servant to the courtyard along with the other vampires, Greylancer noted the two coaches at the ready and asked, "Does not your lord depart by aircraft?"

Zeus and himself aside, he found it odd that Mayerling would choose to go by land. The Capital was less than three hours away by air.

"There seems to be some problem with the propulsion system," the servant answered. "As well, his lordship prefers to travel by coach."

"All of your aircraft?"

"His lordship is in possession of only one vessel."

Greylancer realized now that Mayerling was more old-fashioned than he was.

"Until we meet again," Zeus called and walked out to the landing pad in the courtyard.

"Let us ride together awhile."

When Greylancer turned around, Mayerling was smiling beneath the moonlight.

†

The two coaches rattled down the road side by side for about an hour until they reached a crossroads. Mayerling's coach was a six-horse carriage, compared to Greylancer's two-horse carriage, forcing it to go considerably slower to keep pace.

Greylancer had repeatedly urged Mayerling's driver ahead through the communicator, but the younger Noble insisted on escorting Greylancer until at last they came to the crossroads.

Lowering the window of his coach, Mayerling peered out and smiled. "I wish you a safe journey."

"Will you ride hard to the Capital from here?" Greylancer asked.

Even if he pushed the horses day and night, it would still take three days. It was hardly the way for a man in a hurry. "There is an airport about ten kilometers south of here. There should be several aircraft there."

"Safe travels." Greylancer glanced up at the sky. The moon colored the clouds silver.

Mayerling nodded once.

"Now go," urged Greylancer. "Fare thee well." With this, Greylancer whipped the horses into a gallop.

After watching Greylancer's coach shrink into the distance, the young Noble set out toward his destination like a whirlwind.

When Mayerling had traveled five kilometers south, the wind began to howl.

"My lord." The driver's voice came from the monitor inside the coach. "Our projections were off. It appears Ithaqua comes two weeks earlier this year than last."

"Is it the main front?"

"No. But it will be a considerable trial to go much farther."

"Do not hesitate against what is merely considerable. Go!"

Mayerling listened to the unrelenting rattle of the coach like a cradlesong.

Several minutes later, an invisible force lashed against the side of the coach.

"It's coming!" the driver shouted nervously.

"Ithaqua, come and get me." Mayerling twisted his lips into an invincible smile.

3

After the nuclear war that wiped out humanity, the Nobility created a new world in the image of the past that pulsed through their veins.

The ruins of humanity's metropolises gave way to a vast wilderness stretching as far as the eye could see, dotted with forests and mountains.

The Nobility populated this area with bioengineered beasts and monsters.

Mountains grew arms and legs for moving, rivers surged in different directions, and oceans acquired eyes the size of continents.

Fire-breathing dragons were prey to three-headed birds, while subterranean monsters and goblins fought over the dragon carcasses and blood. All told, the Nobility had dispersed 1,243,0778 monster species throughout the world.

This act begat an unexpected byproduct.

Aside from the Nobility's bioengineered creatures, the evil that once lurked on this planet had stirred back to life.

Most conspicuous were the gods of the four elements, one of which was Ithaqua, the god of wind.

An encounter with this god, whom they knew not how to defeat, posed a greater threat to the Nobility than stakes or knives. Ithaqua did not attempt to destroy the Nobles it encountered.

They were simply taken, never to return, and it was this vanishing act the Nobility feared more than death.

Thud! The wagon shook again.

"My lord, shadows up ahead. About twenty of them."

His eyes trained on the monitor, Mayerling asked, "How do they look? Check their posture and eyes."

"Rounded shoulders. Their eyes burn red."

"Very well. Don't stop. Push past them."

The driver's whip danced, and the coach picked up speed, hurtling against the violent wind.

Their dress identified the shadows as farmers. When the lead horses came within five meters, they scattered right and left with an agility belying their profession.

A single wire was left in their wake, held up about a meter high at both ends.

The cybernetic horses were unable to time their jump. As their legs were swept from under them, the two lead horses flew forward in a brilliant arc, while the rest followed. The coach was no exception; it flipped end over end and crashed down atop the horses.

A split second before impact, the coach's computer activated its defensive program.

Four shock struts sprang out of the corners of the coach and absorbed the impact, then the stabilizer cut loose the horses and righted the coach, landing it gently upright.

The shadows descended upon the coach while it was still airborne.

Closing the six-meter gap in one leap, they pressed up against the coach and banged the sides with their fists.

They were not Nobles, but servants who'd been bitten—"half-humans." While they possessed some of the same physical abilities as Nobles, they lacked the strength to destroy the overseer's transport.

The driver engaged the enemy.

Unstrapping his belt, he grabbed his stake rifle and shot the first three attackers in their hearts.

The fourth and fifth attackers were aiming their crossbows. After taking one arrow in the throat, the driver spat up blood and shot down the fourth attacker before a second arrow caught him dead in the heart.

However, the fifth attacker gaped in disbelief. The arrow had deflected from the driver's chest. The instant the attacker realized the arrow had hit the driver's underarmor, the stake rifle howled, discharging high-pressure gas along with the shot that tore through the half-human. His body turned to dust before it hit the ground.

Meanwhile, a sixth attacker perched atop the coach crept up to the driver from behind. His weapon was a meter-long machete.

Whirling around, the driver leapt onto the coach and sank his teeth into the half-human's carotid artery.

The half-human swung his machete and lopped off the driver's head. The driver, not yet realizing his death, continued to tear into the enemy's neck until first his body, then his head rolled on top of the coach.

When the driver went down at last, the remaining shadows dragged him to the ground, hacked his severed head to pieces with machetes, and skewered his body with countless blades.

The shadows had already accomplished their initial goal.

Without a sound, they leapt away from the coach, lay low, and waited for the fruits of their labor.

A fragmentation bomb placed beneath the coach exploded and engulfed the transport in scarlet flames.

When the flames and blast threatened to consume them, the shadows scrambled to safer ground.

A dark silhouette wavered in the colorful flames.

When the fire-drowned mass lurched away from the coach, the shadows let out voiceless screams. The ten-thousand-degree heat should have incinerated even a Noble's bones.

Suddenly, the dark figure collapsed and was swallowed by the flames once again. When the half-humans saw this, triumphant smiles appeared on their rough faces. Only six of them remained.

It quickly became four. Something had stretched out from the fire, sliced off the heads of the two lead attackers in one sideways swing and cut across their chests on the return.

The survivors did not understand what had happened. What they saw was a human hand sticking out from the flames. With the fingers in a line like a blade, the hand slashed right.

Two more heads rolled on the right.

"Mayerling's claw…" groaned one of the remaining two. They had received orders to kill Mayerling before he wielded it.

The hand rose again. Out of the flames rose Mayerling, his purple cape swirling in the superheated wind currents.

The flames of death, falling away from his cape with one shake, had not burned any part of his skin or mane.

Against the flames consuming the coach in the background the figure appeared strangely still, as though it existed in a different world.

Here stood Vlijmen Mayerling, overseer of the Western Frontier sector.

"If I have incurred the enmity of my people, then I am to blame. But this does not appear to be the case. Whom do you serve?" Was this the voice of the same man that had been consumed in flames just now? How gentle he sounded. Like the sound of snow falling on the Holy Night.

Mayerling stepped toward the shadows.

His steps were fainter than the sound of falling snow.

Shaaah! The shadows bared their fangs.

But they were unable to move. Paralyzed by the handsome, young vampire's aura, their bodies were numb to their bones.

"Can you not speak?" Mayerling extended a hand and beckoned the shadows closer. His fingers were slender and beautiful like those of a woman. "Then come closer."

The shadows began to walk without hesitation. They ambled closer to the Noble as if they'd lost the will to resist.

"Perhaps now I can hear you. Now speak. Which master do you serve?"

Their lips began to move. The shadows attempted to utter a name.

The moon caught a glint of metal in the darkness.

Before the crack of the gunshot reached anyone's ears, one shadow's head shattered to pieces, and another shadow fell over in a spray of blood.

Mayerling.

He had expected an unceasing barrage of bullets.

The Noble held up a hand in front of his handsome face.

When a tiny hole appeared in the palm, he swung the hand downward and—

A lead bullet hot enough to vaporize his blood burrowed into the black earth.

Turning his head just a hint, Mayerling stared into the distant darkness. It was unmistakably the direction from which the bullet had come.

But only for an instant, as he turned in the direction of the burning coach.

A tall shadow stood there. Behind him loomed an enormous tree, in the shadow of which he'd likely been lurking.

But Mayerling's eyes were drawn to the two swords strapped in a crisscross behind the shadow's back.

The rough-hewn hilts protruding from either side of his head were quivering.

Trying to suppress his surprise, the shadow said in a low, low voice, "I'm trembling with excitement. You felled those humans in two swings. Perhaps you *are* qualified to rule as overseer."

"Are you with the sharpshooter?" Mayerling made a loose fist. When he opened it, the bullet wound on his palm was gone.

"The damn gunner failed. I didn't want to go along with his dirty trick to begin with. Now you shall suffer the might of the Streda, a style of swordsmanship I have practiced to defeat you Nobles."

"So there will be no more bullets." The wind coaxed a faint smile over Mayerling's lips.

The bullet he'd caught in his palm was supposed to have crushed his face and head. As ineffective as the attack was against Nobles, it would have taken at least a few seconds for Mayerling to recover completely, allowing the tall swordsman to close in and pierce his heart.

But Mayerling had caught the first bullet, and a second did not follow. With the reason still unknown, another battle was about to unfold in the depths of night lit only by the moon.

"Allow me to introduce myself. I am the swordsman Shizam. Take that name with you to the netherworld."

"Then see that you do not forget your name," said Mayerling. The white fangs peering from his lips gleamed in the moonlight.

†

The gunner had waited for his chance in the bushes just below the northbound road.

He had readied three rifles. He had also brought thirty bullets with him, but if all had gone according to plan, one would have sufficed.

Yet he had wasted two bullets to silence a confession. *Good for nothing bumpkins! At least you'll go to your graves regretting how you lost your worthless lives!*

Because his rifles were antiquated flintlocks, in which the powder and ball were loaded through the muzzle and the powder ignited in the flashpan with flint, he was not able to fire repeated shots. That was his greatest weakness. But his long-range marksmanship, perhaps more accurately called remote marksmanship, more than compensated for this weakness. In fact, the distance to his intended target had measured more than ten kilometers.

But at present, he could only tremble with fear. The target crystal at his feet projected an image—his lethal shot had missed. No, it had been blocked.

"Impossible!" he'd told himself a hundred times over.

The skills he'd acquired through dreadful, diligent toil enabled him to shoot down a butterfly fluttering about at one end of the continent from the other side.

And yet that Noble had...

This first-ever blunder had caused him to forget himself. By the time he had grabbed another rifle, loaded the powder and lead bullet in the muzzle, and poured the gunpowder into the flashpan, a full minute had elapsed since his miss. His distraction had caused him to overlook another extraordinary mistake.

When finally he took aim and cocked the hammer holding the flint, there was a voice: "A magic shot. First I've seen a human practice it. From the direction the muzzle is pointed, your target is a traveler heading toward the Capital. Who employed you to kill the overlord of the West?"

The gunner spun around at lightning speed.

Before he could pull the trigger, the rifle was snatched away from him, and the gunstock swung up and smashed against his chin.

Next to the callow gunner lying on his back, Greylancer stood, momentarily absorbed by the rifle. Then he glared in the direction the rifle had been pointed. "It appears you have many enemies, Mayerling."

CHAPTER 7:
DUCHESS MIRCALLA

1

Greylancer returned to Bistoria, the regional capital of his sector of the Frontier, three days later.

Five minutes after boarding a gyrocopter at the border checkpoint, Greylancer returned to his castle, where a shocking piece of news awaited.

Mayerling had wielded his evil claw and grievously injured Chancellor Cornelius inside the halls of the Privy Council Ministry.

"You have orders to report at once," said the chief steward.

Though Old Cornelius did not perish, he was still being treated in the Nobles' own hospital, where science and magic met.

"I expected nothing less," Greylancer said with a smile.

This same smile floated to his lips once again, when Vice-Chancellor Pitaka issued Greylancer his orders:

"Lord Greylancer, I've been waiting for you. Mayerling has returned to his sector, following his attack on Chancellor Cornelius. He will likely hole up in his castle and engage our army there. The Privy Council has appointed you subcommander of the counterinsurgency forces."

"Who is the commander?"

"Duchess Mircalla of the Southern Frontier sector." A faint smile came over Greylancer's lips, at which Vice-Chancellor Pitaka glared and quickly added, "Your army will assemble tomorrow. Best you go to the War Ministry to meet with Mircalla immediately. You two will have full operational control."

"I must ask. What has become of the engagement against the OSB?"

"The Privy Council holds your command and victory on the moon base in high regard. Consider this appointment as subcommander as an expression of our appreciation. If you return having performed your duty, I have every expectation that more accolades will follow."

"What of the OSB vanguard?" he pressed.

Whether Vice-Chancellor Pitaka recognized the force behind the question was not apparent in his expressionless face. "If you've returned to your sector, then you received the government decree. The plasma attack on suspected OSB enclaves was originally set for tomorrow. In light of the rebel insurgency, however, zero hour has been pushed to three days after Mayerling's surrender."

†

When Greylancer arrived at the counterinsurgency head-quarters taking up a corner of the spacious War Ministry, the awestruck faces of the officers, and the beguiling smile of the duchess, greeted him.

"Lord Greylancer, it has been too long," Mircalla said.

"Indeed."

Mircalla's smile turned affectionate, like that of a mother admonishing a mischievous urchin. *He is as unsociable as he was a millennium ago*, she thought. The faint scent of fragrance tickled the warrior's nostrils.

"Given the sudden turn of events, we haven't much time. What is the plan?"

The moonlight filtering in through the window illuminated the two overseers and officers. The walls were hewn stone, the room devoid of computers and machines.

Mircalla crooked a pale finger as if to beckon.

The space near the ceiling sparked to life, and an image of the moon suddenly appeared.

"The headquarters have already been fitted to your needs, I see."

"Yes, excuse me." Her finger, adorned with a diamond ring of a size that might be mistaken for the moon itself, danced in the air, and the moon image melted, giving way to a map of a vast land. "The Western Frontier sector, Lord Greylancer. " Despite having been appointed commander, Mircalla maintained a tone of respect toward her subcommander. Greylancer's glorious military service and skill as overseer demanded it, to say nothing of the reality that no one dared oppose him. "The key departments have already determined the composition of the troops. With this in mind, the strategy I have devised is the following."

The map transformed into a three-dimensional graphic.

In the air were bombers, while on the ground were missile tanks, giant mechanized infantry, and a battalion of regular infantry.

Greylancer grabbed a bomber in his hand and took a good look. It was a saucer-shaped object about three centimeters in diameter. The actual aircraft measured fifty meters. "How many?" he asked.

"Fifty bombers."

"Missile tanks?"

"Fifty. As well as a hundred giant infantry and a thousand regular infantry."

"A tricky business—punishing a Noble." Greylancer returned the aircraft and smiled bitterly. "If we fire an antiproton missile from the Capital, the entire Western Frontier sector will be destroyed. But it would not kill a single Noble."

"Yes, wooden stakes, steel swords, sharp arrows are the only effective weapons in bringing us down in any age."

"In order to destroy Mayerling, we must penetrate the castle walls and rely on the infantry's swords and lances and bows. Mayerling will not sit back quietly. A frontal attack of the likes outlined on this map will spell heavy damage for our side."

"The central government has already anticipated as much."

"Are the giant mechanized and regular infantries comprised of androids?"

Mircalla shook her head slowly. The gold hair clip and diamond-studded crimson dress sparkled in the moonlight. "The giants are AI, and the regular infantry comprised of half-human soldiers."

"Your proposed attack will cause untold fatalities."

"Odd…" Mircalla touched a finger to her lips and smiled. Her fangs flashed beneath her lips; they were snaggleteeth unbecoming a duchess. She, too, fed upon human blood. "The Greylancer that I know would feel no compunction over sacrificing his subjects in order to carry out his purpose. He is a true Noble among Nobles."

"To carry out a purpose," he affirmed quietly. "But those sacrifices were ones of necessity. They died for a just cause. They have never been sent to their deaths for my self-interest, nor for senseless wars."

"Such misguided—or shall I say, compassionate—thinking." Mircalla dropped her head respectfully. "If you have objections to my proposed strategy, I would welcome hearing them."

"No, I believe this is the best strategy."

"I'm pleased to have your approval."

"But *this* will be the outcome." Greylancer moved toward Mayerling's castle. The scale holograph of the battlefield stretched twenty meters long and ten meters wide. "I shall defend the castle." With a grumble, he said, "Commence your attack."

Mircalla answered with a nod.

†

"I don't believe it," said Mircalla, her voice filled with shock. "That my army would be so easily defeated as this."

"Not defeated. Annihilated." Greylancer cast a frigid look down at the dead troops and tanks lying in ruins on the holographic battlefield, then craned his neck to the right and left.

His joints cracked. Flames and black smoke rose up in the air. They were holographic, of course, but they would burn you if you touched them. "This is the outcome I foresee based on the arsenal Mayerling has at his disposal. The strategy was mine, but I expect Mayerling to employ a similar one. But beware, Mircalla. He may have weapons of which we have no knowledge."

"How could he procure such things?"

"Built clandestine factories and hired able technicians, perhaps. He may well have contrived the weapons himself. Your failure to consider this possibility, Mircalla, suggests you've become too accustomed to your own idleness."

The bewitching beauty gnashed her teeth. Not out of self-reproach or regret. A look of hate had spread over her face, and she cast an upward glance at Greylancer. "If this is the best strategy, then what is next best?"

"I do not know," grumbled Greylancer. "I leave now for my sister's. You may call on me anytime."

"With pleasure," said Mircalla, bowing again.

Greylancer nodded and strode away.

When the sound of his footsteps faded, Duchess Mircalla dismissed the officers and gazed up at the moon in the window. "May you never learn, Lord Greylancer," the supreme commander of the counterinsurgency force and overseer of the Southern Frontier sector intoned like a curse, "that our foe this time is not Mayerling alone. Dear friend Zeus—beloved Macula, pray that we will be able to achieve our purpose. Nay, we must seize victory with our own hands. And tear away their flesh and blood with these two hands."

Her fists trembled with anger and hatred.

Shaahh! The duchess hissed, her right hand slashing down the front of her dress.

The fabric tore open and fell around her feet.

The moon gazed down at the woman's naked body.

"Mayerling."

Her right hand danced, its motion like an elegant dance.

A red line streaked from the left side of her neck and diagonally down her lustrous right breast, and quickly turned into a thick cascade of blood.

"Greylancer."

Her left hand leapt.

A second blood streak ran down her other breast, forming a condemning cross.

"Watch me, dear Zeus. I shall send any enemy that stands in our way to their end. Like this!"

Whether driven to madness by the brilliant moon or having simply become too incensed, Mircalla smeared the dripping blood over her entire body.

Her breasts shook; her glistening stomach swayed.

The blood spread over her face.

And then, the duchess lifted a hand and suckled on her blood-stained finger.

In the dark where only the moonlight and the woman's body glowed, the sound that would drive a Noble to rapture echoed across the stone room.

†

The coach, arranged for Greylancer by the central government, traveled thirty minutes west on the road and passed through the mansion gates of Greylancer's childhood home.

Greylancer alighted from the coach in the courtyard, where the chief steward, house staff, and a young couple stood in a line before him.

Whereas the wife appeared to be in her early twenties, the husband was not much younger than Greylancer. However, he cut a diminutive figure that was a far cry from Greylancer's stately mien.

This was Greylancer's only family: younger sister Laria and her husband Count Brueghel. Though he himself was from a family of pedigree, having been stripped of his estate and rank from past failings, Brueghel now lived here, having essentially been taken in by the bride's family.

"Seems you're having a bit of a day." Laria cast her stately brother a look filled with both sarcasm and unabated reverence.

After bowing and lightly kissing the palm of her outstretched hand, Greylancer muttered, "A day indeed," and acknowledged his brother-in-law with a nod, failing, despite his best effort, to smile. He did not get along with Brueghel, who was an officer working in the Civil Administration Bureau.

Yet on this day, the oft-stolid Brueghel returned a cordial smile.

When Laria teased her husband later by asking "What got into you back there?" Brueghel replied, "It was your brother. He had an odd kindness in his eyes."

The three went into the sitting room, where Brueghel said, "I beg your pardon, but I have some urgent business to attend to," and excused himself.

"I'm sorry, Brother," said Laria. "Something came up at work."

"I thought civil servants were anything but busy."

"He's gone to give a poetry lecture to schoolkids," Laria said with an air of indifference, expecting her brother to jeer.

Yet the answer she heard was *Oh?* Laria nearly threw her head back in amazement, detecting even a hint of respect in his voice. "That suits him. Brueghel must be very pleased."

Greylancer was aware of Brueghel's ambition to be a poet. She had expected her brother's laughter to ring across the room. Yet his tone was nothing if not gentle. It was enough for Laria to suspect whether this man might not be an OSB impersonator.

2

"How is *it* working?" Laria filled Greylancer's silver glass with the blood-wine brought to them by a steward, glancing expectedly for a favorable reply.

"It is a great help." Greylancer raised his left hand and tilted the gold urn-shaped ring in her direction. There were three tiny holes on what appeared to be a lid. A good look revealed white plumes of smoke rising out of the ring. "Thanks to this *time-deceiving incense* you invented, I know now the reality of day."

That Greylancer could scour the sector on his chariot to wipe out the OSB threat night and day was due to Laria's invention. Anyone inhaling its scent experiences the illusion that night is day, and day is night. Thus when Greylancer walked in the light of day, his subjective experience was of being awake and active at night.

"The counterinsurgency force will be deployed to the Western Frontier sector tomorrow. Best you do not go out today."

"Yes, I've heard what's happened. But this is awfully sudden."

"We are dealing with a ruler of his own sector. I fear we may even be too late, given our adversary. In many ways, Lord Vlijmen Mayerling is more formidable than any of the other overseers."

"Even you, Brother?" Laria's eyes opened wide.

"He has won the support of his people. Something none of the other three overseers have been able to accomplish, including myself."

"But what of it?" Noble that she was, the significance of this fact escaped her. "The humans will not make a bit of difference in a battle between Nobles, regardless of their adoration of Mayerling. Isn't that so?"

Greylancer fell silent for a moment, and then answered, "Indeed, you're right."

"You're not acting like yourself," Laria asked. "Is something the matter?"

"No—has there been any discord between Chancellor Cornelius and Mayerling in the past?"

"Of course," she said with a nod. "The government probably only gave you a formal briefing…" The brows knitted on her feline face as she began to explain. "Mayerling attacked Chancellor Cornelius after the chancellor had laughed off his protest of the operation to wipe out the OSB infiltrators—or so it's been reported. But if Mayerling were so quick-tempered to reach for his weapon, the Western Frontier would have perished long ago. No, dear Brother—there is a plan to remove the overseers from power in the Frontier, and Chancellor Cornelius is its architect."

"That's absurd. Our absolute managerial rights were awarded directly by the Sacred Ancestor himself. Not even the government dares tamper with those rights."

"It has been six thousand one hundred years since the Sacred Ancestor disappeared from sight. His influence was bound to fade."

"Is that what you think?"

"Not I, no."

"The chancellor must be in league with someone more powerful than the Sacred Ancestor. Neither he nor this unknown faction would attempt to rise up in defiance otherwise."

"That's for certain," she said with a grim smile.

"Any idea whom it might be?"

"I haven't a clue." Her smile vanished.

It was an ironclad rule of Noble society—no one dared face down Greylancer's grave expression with anything but trepidation.

"No matter, all will be made plain in due time. Now then, I am in need of weapons."

Her look darkening, Laria said, "Oh, yes…that's right," as if to remind herself. "Varossa has built many interesting…devices. You should try them out."

"If they are Varossa's, by all means. Can we go at once?"

"Of course."

†

Several minutes later, Greylancer and Laria had made their way inside a marble dome towering over the courtyard.

A single moonbeam cascaded in like a waterfall from on high, a great distance away. There appeared to be a window somewhere.

Bathed in light, countless devices and vehicles of compelling shape and obscure function cast shadows dancing in the vast workspace below.

Elegantly designed stairs and slopes ran vertically and sideways with great mathematical accuracy, connecting various workspaces and gravity stabilizers suspended throughout the cavernous space.

"Varossa," Laria called out. Before the echoes of the master weaponsmith's name faded into silence, a figure wearing a turquoise cape and a ring-shaped antigrav belt around his waist swooped down from above.

"If it isn't Lord Greylancer," said the dour-faced man. Varossa was a few years younger than Greylancer, but older than Brueghel. But from his crest of silver hair alone, he might be mistaken for a man hundreds of years old. "Chatting with your long-neglected sister, were you? You are a warrior of the most regrettable kind. I dream of the days of our Sacred Ancestor, when a battle-weary warrior would have attended to repairing or exchanging their damaged shields, broken lances, and chipped swords before seeking rest or commiseration."

Laria's face turned pale, while a bitter smile came across Greylancer's lips. "You're exactly right, Varossa. But have you anything new to satisfy me?"

"Well, this is an odd question. If any of my creations have ever failed your standards, I shall cut off my head on this very spot. Of course, your eye for such things has always been a bit cloudy, unlike your father." As he delivered his spittle-laden remark, Varossa's eyes were fixed in a hard stare. Seeing the contented expression on Greylancer's face, however, he came back into himself. "Forgive me, my lord. How can I help you?"

"I'm looking for a chariot."

"As you wish. But first—" He pointed to the antigrav belts on hand.

Greylancer and Laria opened the rings and closed the belts around their waists. Then they needed only point the road reader toward their destination.

The three began to rise and soon hovered about a meter over the platform and, after flying on about two hundred meters, landed about five to six meters below.

They had descended to the Greylancer family's weapons block. The entire arsenal had been designed and manufactured by Varossa himself.

Greylancer took in and marveled at the spectacle surrounding him.

Row upon row of chariots of every size; lances, long swords, and short swords hanging from racks; stockpiles of shields, cutting-edge power suits, and old-fashioned plate armor. This horrible scene stretched as far as the eye could see, past the horizon. This arsenal alone could arm a division of a thousand men for battle.

"You've added to your stock," said Greylancer.

Varossa nodded quietly. "They've all been enhanced as well. Now, what manner of contraption are you in need of? If you can try to imagine it with that feeble head of yours." The weapon-smith pressed an index finger to Greylancer's temple.

Weapons and arms of every variety flashed across Greylancer's vision. A data injection. Greylancer's brain streamed the data for tens of thousands of items.

In a fraction of a second, an image of a particular chariot flashed to mind.

"Ah, yes, that'll do." With a nod of Varossa's head, a thread of light fell from the ceiling.

Suddenly, a chariot materialized where the light landed on the floor.

The chariot was the same size and shape as the one Greylancer had lost in the moon battle.

"The force field is twice as powerful as the previous model's. You should be able to penetrate any of the OSB's defense fields and charge into enemy territory."

"*Should* is unacceptable."

"Then by all means, see for yourself." Varossa gestured toward the chariot with an unshakeable smile.

"Very well." Greylancer climbed onto Varossa's beloved invention.

Stepping onto the platform, he felt the force field envelop the vehicle.

"See how you fare against the weakest foe." Varossa tapped his thigh with his index finger.

Another thread of light dropped from the sky—

Which was no doubt connected to a multitude of God-given items.

An OSB ground vehicle the Nobles had begun calling a thunder tank materialized before Greylancer, several meters away.

The tank, easily three times larger than Greylancer's chariot, hulked over the Noble, looking as if it might crush him at any moment.

Looking around the stockpile of weapons and machinery surrounding them, Varossa grunted, "Out of the way," and putting a foot on one of the chariots nearby, pushed it sideways.

The chariot and the rest of the weapons and arms in view slid back till they vanished completely out of sight.

Inside the cavernous hall, only Laria, Varossa, the thunder tank, Greylancer, and the chariot remained. And murderous intent.

3

The massive stockpile cramming the floor had all been a 3D hologram.

Greylancer nodded at Varossa, unflinching.

"The thunder tank will act and react exactly as if the OSB were operating it. It will shoot to kill. If you lose, you will also perish, Lord Greylancer. Is that understood?"

"I expect nothing less."

"Good." No sooner had he said it than the OSB tank rumbled toward Greylancer.

The Noble felt the platform shake underfoot as the chariot hummed to life.

Just as the enormous tank rolled within a meter of Greylancer's chariot, it crashed into the force field, flipping head over end in the air.

Landing on its side, the tank spun around in a circle like a helpless insect until it righted itself and retreated without a sound.

One silver ball, a second, and then a third shot out from the three barrels extending from the tank's gun turret.

Greylancer swung the chariot right and evaded the first two shots, but the third hit the force field.

The silver projectile was an artillery shell measuring thirty centimeters.

The outer shell splintered away, while its contents grazed Greylancer's head and disappeared behind him.

Within the shells were steel spikes about five centimeters thick.

"Now let's double the force field." Greylancer closed in on the tank, evading the incoming cannon fire.

The enemy circled right and fired more shells.

When one shell smashed through the floor near her feet, Laria let out a shriek.

Suddenly, Greylancer's chariot took to the air and cut a diagonal path toward the tank. The Noble had switched to gravitational propulsion.

The OSB computer faltered for a split second. Unable to calculate an evasive maneuver, the computer rotated the tank's turret and fired a random shot.

Though the shell hit the chariot head-on, both the casing and spikes were deflected from the armor.

Switching off the force-field generator, Greylancer whirled atop the enemy's gun turret.

His right arm rose skyward.

The silver lance in his hand came down like a lightning bolt.

As soon as the blade slashed through the thunder from top to bottom, Greylancer jumped back onto his chariot.

A red streak tore across the contours of the tank, growing thicker and thicker until the armor ruptured and exploded. A massive fireball swallowed Greylancer and swept across the ground and sky.

The scene was strangely quiet.

Nearly ten seconds passed before the fire consumed the tank and went out.

Greylancer and the chariot appeared above the black ruins like a dream.

Laria ran to her brother. "Why must you be so reckless?"

"Well, is the chariot to your liking?" Varossa asked politely.

"It is a fine chariot."

"Naturally," said the weaponsmith, cocking his head with a self-satisfied smile.

"Why didn't you equip every chariot with the superior force field to begin with?" Laria asked, an edge in her voice.

"There was no predicting what the enemy was capable of."

"But we have engaged this type of OSB tank in battle more than once."

An indescribable look of horror came over Varossa's face. "Are you perhaps suggesting that I might be lying?"

"I'm sold," said Greylancer, electing not to answer. "I shall ride this chariot tomorrow morning. See that you get it ready." After handing down this order like only a Noble could, Greylancer switched on the antigrav belt and floated away, his sister following in his wake.

†

Watching Greylancer and Laria leave, Varossa grumbled quietly to himself at the door, "He distrusts even this weaponsmith, who has served House Greylancer for five thousand years. Such banality. A worthless master." And then a broad smile came across Varossa's face as he continued. "I would have expected nothing less from my master—Lord Greylancer. A mere grub of a son that you are compared to your father, you shall have my grudging support and these skills honed over five millennia. Long life and well-being, my lord."

The next day, the counterinsurgency forces departed for the

deadly battleground.

Since the troops couldn't very well proceed down the road in a convoy, the army boarded a cargo vessel and within three hours arrived in the Western Frontier sector—Mayerling's dominion.

In a siege such as this one, a gravitational barrier typically shielded the castle, Nobles' residences, and the strategic headquarters. The initial attack necessarily involved attempting to destroy the barrier.

But Duchess Mircalla, the supreme commander of the counterinsurgency forces, could only blink in disbelief upon hearing the analysis reports from the aerial reconnaissance sensors.

"As unconventional as the Western Frontier overseer may be, it's impossible that he is shielding his entire dominion with a gravitational barrier! It can't be done without the Capital's galactic energy changer." This was Thorzak Yanzarlai, a duke of the Eastern Frontier sector.

"Then Mayerling must have procured a copy of the very same device," said Mircalla, having already regained her composure. Glancing at Greylancer with her blue pools, she said, "You're awfully calm. Why is that?"

"No reason. Only that I have always believed anything is possible—things that both the Nobility and humanity might struggle to fathom."

"How very mindful of you." Mircalla turned to the data projected in the air. "According to the data, the barrier's strength is a hundred quadrillion joules—nearly enough power to keep the barrier up and running for eternity. We are nowhere unless we dispense with this barrier first."

"So a full-force assault would require some time…then how about the age-old tactic of starving out the enemy?" remarked Lieutenant General Dreyse Ghishirshin of the Capital Defense Division, in jest. Though the strategist's record against the OSB was unblemished, he had an unfortunate knack for souring the mood with his arrogance. When no one laughed, he winced.

Needless to say, human blood was the Nobility's—

vampires'—source of sustenance. This supply, collected both willingly and unwillingly from the local population, not only sated the Nobility's appetites, but also filled frozen or otherwise dried and pressure-packed storage units scattered across the land.

A year's worth of blood was typically kept on hand in any Noble castle.

In addition, Mayerling had perfected a cocktail of mineral-infused synthetic blood that tasted much like the real thing. He manufactured it in large quantities in a factory near the castle. A prolonged siege of a year or two years was exactly what Mayerling desired.

Of course, Lt. General Ghishirshin had quipped about starving the enemy, knowing so. Yet the members of the war council remained still as stone.

"Every castle floorplan includes secret evacuation tunnels, but the possibility of escape is rendered nil since the entire territory has been shielded by the barrier. No escape, no entry. It will be a long, drawn-out war." Scanning the data, General Lei Huo Chao took a drag from his pipe. He was an elite strategist from the War Ministry. Given his background, perhaps he was well suited for a long-term conflict.

"That will not be the case."

The generals, who'd resigned themselves to a protracted campaign, made no attempt to hide their anger or disbelief toward the voice of dissent. "Just what is it you mean, Lord Greylancer?"

"You possess some stratagem against Lord Mayerling?"

"What I possess is an understanding of Mayerling's character." Greylancer extended his left arm.

The image of a Noble appeared.

"Mayerling?" Despite recognizing it was nothing more than a hologram, the generals looked aghast, partially thanks to how lifelike the young Noble appeared, and partially due to the fear he inspired.

"Behold his face," said Greylancer, jerking his chin at the handsome face. "His lineage, rank, and record are beyond question.

You can recognize a warrior by his look alone. Do not be fooled by his handsomeness. His is a face to fear, Commander."

"Agreed," Mircalla answered flatly. "His fierce will for a fight, incisiveness, and ample confidence." She addressed the hologram. "How did you come by these qualities, Mayerling? This is the face of the enemy that we must fight. No doubt, you will stand your ground to the very end. What clever gambit will you try?"

"His only option is to wait out the siege. We need only come up with an anti-barrier to neutralize his defenses. Far better than suffering casualties through needless skirmishes. Mayerling may have played right into our hand." This was General Sade Jermyn, General Lei Huo Chao's colleague and the number two man in the War Ministry. A standout in a ministry derided for their armchair strategists, he was recognized as one who piloted his own aircraft.

"Who do you think you're dealing with?" Greylancer scoffed. To the battle-weary warrior, Jermyn was nothing more than an untested general, an impostor trying to pass as a hero. Despite the general's sneer, Greylancer continued, "Look at his eyes. The jaw. This is the face of a man who will lead his men into enemy territory himself. Such a man will not be content to hole up in his castle and play a waiting game. Open your eyes. The moment we let down our guard, he will strike us with his army—a cunning attack that we cannot even imagine."

"You're an impudent one," seethed Jermyn, baring his teeth. His fangs gleamed in the moonlight streaming into the war room. "You are speculating without substance. What knowledge have you about Mayerling? Grow up together, did you?"

"Today may well be our first encounter."

"Do you mean to mock me, Greylancer?"

A murderous air that made the warriors want to turn away swept across the room. Jermyn shot to his feet.

"That's enough, both of you!" The voice of the supreme commander immobilized Jermyn. "As long as I am commander, I will not have any infighting. If you desire bloodshed, let it be Mayerling's."

On the battlefield, a superior's command was ironclad.

Jermyn sat down in indignation as Greylancer stifled a smile.

"The Privy Council's orders are to end this conflict within five days. Time enough left to our own devices," said Mircalla, smiling. Had she been entrusted as overseer on pedigree alone, the duchess would lack the wherewithal to manage the Frontier. "At any rate, let us put forth our best efforts. Lord Greylancer, can you verify your assessment?"

"No, it is solely my assessment of Mayerling. But make no mistake, anyone with a passing glance of Mayerling, even from a distance, would concur."

"As much as I'd like to agree with you, that alone will not do. General Jermyn, I believe yours is the most sensible course of action. But we haven't time for a drawn-out war. Have you a strategy to cross swords with Mayerling within five days?"

Jermyn distorted what was already reputed a menacing face and closed his eyes in deep contemplation. The battle-tested warrior and master strategist thrived in times like these. Smiling, he opened his eyes almost immediately and nodded, "Yes, I do."

CHAPTER 8:
RAIN OF JAVELINS

1

A most distressing incident befell the counterinsurgency forces early next morning.

At daybreak, Mayerling lowered the gravitational barrier shielding his dominion and fired a torrent of javelins over the camp.

Because the barrier encircling Mayerling's dominion did not quite stretch over the entire sector, the troops were encamped just inside the border's perimeter. Thus not one javelin had landed outside in neighboring territory. The javelins, which the counterinsurgents effortlessly fended off, measured three meters long, five centimeters around, and weighed five hundred kilograms. Falling at twelve hundred meters per second, they hit with a thousand tons of force on impact.

And yet the damage inflicted was minimal. The innumerable javelins had merely fallen like an endless volley of arrows around the encampments protected by gravitational barriers, around the super-alloy coffins of the Nobles.

The Nobility also employed once-bitten half-humans and androids to guard against day raids by human resisters. Whereas the javelins felled these servants outside the barrier, the Nobility's weapons and materiel went undamaged.

After the first wave of attacks subsided, three minutes passed before the second wave split the clouds and poured down from the sky. Greylancer appeared under the sun.

The ground was riddled with gleaming black javelins as still more deadly blades were repelled by barriers and fell feebly about Greylancer's feet.

The javelins coming within meters of Greylancer ricocheted away from the Noble. It was the work of his long lance. Greylancer twirled the lance in his right hand almost casually, flicking away every javelin that fell in his path.

As soon as Mayerling's domain lowered its barrier, counter-insurgent sensors returned fire. Countless arrows shot into the horizon from the camp toward Mayerling's castle.

Oddly enough, Mayerling chose not to launch nuclear missiles. A heat-based attack was ineffectual against the Nobility, and human fatalities were of little consequence to the Nobles who regarded the mortals as no better than insects.

The rain continued. The waves of javelins blacked out the sky from the distant horizon to Mayerling's castle overlooking the hills a thousand kilometers away.

"Well played, Mayerling. You've effectively avoided any cause for complaint by any of the territories, no matter who may be in league with whom. As well, this rain of javelins is a demonstration of your strength."

A security vehicle approached, weaving and steamrolling past the thicket of javelins on the ground, and stopped next to Greylancer.

Four half-humans, wearing black-visored helmets, stepped out of the vehicle.

While able to roam about in the light of day, these once-bitten humans were vulnerable to sunlight, requiring them to be covered in blackout gear from head to toe.

"My lord, you must seek cover!"

"It's too dangerous!"

They were the only words they managed to get out before the next volley of javelins impaled them from back to front.

So sudden was their end that they each continued several steps toward Greylancer before falling dead at his feet.

"Fools—serves you right," he spat out, and then he summoned a trio of AG—Android Giants.

Three androids standing three meters tall emerged from the encampment. They approached, brandishing their long swords and striking down the javelins raining down from above, filling the air with the sound of metal clanging against metal. The AGs stopped before Greylancer.

"See that the bodies are buried." It was an order that would have stunned anyone who knew the Noble.

Regardless of the devotion with which half-humans served their master, in death, they were cast aside like so much monster fodder. Such was the fate of half-humans. Yet the Nobility's greatest warrior had just now ordered a proper burial for the dead.

The AG carried the bodies away, and the javelin attack ended soon after.

An invisible shield went up over Mayerling's territory again.

"My chariot!" The half-humans were the only ones to hear Greylancer's call resounding through the camp.

Seconds later, only the wind witnessed the chariot tear through the seemingly unbreakable barrier and blaze a path above the wintry plains.

†

There were no responses to his incursion, and in less than a minute, Greylancer landed on the eastern edge of a village a mere stone's throw from Mayerling's castle.

"A necessary flight, I'm afraid. Circumstances what they are, it couldn't be helped. There isn't time to lose. But first—" Greylancer alighted from the chariot and strode toward the village.

Not a soul could be found on the sun-drenched road. He had no choice but to force his way in. Greylancer had not satiated his thirst the night before and was parched.

A house came into view from between the trees.

The Noble bristled at the sound of the turning waterwheel. That the Nobility disliked running water was a fact known throughout the land.

"I have no choice."

The other houses were quite a distance away and likely located riverside. Even in his state of dormancy, Mayerling would certainly be alerted to any trouble in town. What Greylancer desired was a surreptitious encounter. Mayerling was not yet aware of Greylancer's encroachment into Western territory, thanks to the chariot's stealth program, which allowed him to pass undetected by both radar and clairvoyance. This was another invention that Laria had conceptualized and Varossa created.

When Greylancer was a mere ten paces away from the house, the door opened and through it emerged a girl of about sixteen or seventeen and her mother.

They sighted the giant in front of them before anything else.

Their shock gave way to suspicion, and as their expressions arrived at terror, Greylancer strode forward.

A Noble's presence alone was enough to paralyze humans where they stood. At least in Greylancer's experience.

But this mother and daughter were exceptions. The emotion that broke through the fear and burst out of their mouths was pure anger.

"A Noble!"

"An enemy of Lord Mayerling," said the mother. Then she called out, "Dear!"

Seconds passed. The door flew open again, and out rushed two men—a boy in his early twenties and his father this time. The scythe and long barrel in their hands as well as the wailing siren explained their delay.

"You must be with the invading army! You're not getting a step past us."

"If you're aiming for the castle, you're going to have to kill us all! Take this," the father said and handed the women a hatchet and a wooden stake.

Arching a brow, Greylancer said, "Seeing how you've armed your wife and daughter, it appears you value Mayerling more than your family. Is that true of all humans in the West?"

"No ruler cares more about his people than Lord Mayerling. He's saved the lives of every one of us here. No, that goes for the entire village. We might as well be dead. We'll gladly give our lives for him." The father was trembling, and his face was dripping with sweat as if to affirm the genuineness of his brave intentions.

Greylancer turned his gaze on the girl. "You too?"

"Yes, that's right," said the girl, with a hint of innocence still about her even as she nodded sharply. Suddenly, Greylancer realized why he'd felt something was amiss. Teeth chattering in fear, the girl continued, "When Mother and Father were afflicted with a mysterious bacteria that began to rot away their flesh, Lord Mayerling came from the castle himself to deliver the medicine. Both my parents—and my brother and I—when we became infected, he saved us. Even though most of the village fell ill, no one had to die. Afterward, we were also able to receive periodic exams. Lord Mayerling saved our lives."

"I came to this land fifty years ago." It was the mother's turn to speak. "In other parts of the Frontier, children and babies that could have been saved with a little food and medicine died by the dozens at the slightest outbreak of disease. The rulers did nothing but take our blood. Some kind of rulers they are! They can't even protect their own people! When I came here, I thought I'd died and gone to heaven. Fifty years—fifty years living here is plenty. I won't let you lay a finger on Lord Mayerling."

"Did you ever live in the North?" Greylancer asked.

"No, just South and East."

"Hmm." Greylancer looked upon the girl. "When I look upon your faces, they are different from those of humans living in the other sectors, including my own. Your faces are peaceful. Do you also credit Mayerling for this?"

'That's right," answered the girl's father, nodding. "The people of this sector live with smiles on their faces. Sure life is hard, but we will never starve or freeze from cold. We aren't forbidden from having festivals, either That's why the people here have peace of mind. Try visiting any other sector of the Frontier. You can't get even a newborn to laugh. Life's so hard and bitter that there isn't a soul able to smile. A land where its children are just as scared as the adults isn't any place to live. Well? What about your land? Do the children laugh there?"

"Hm…" *Mayerling, that favormonger,* thought Greylancer. *Listen to how brazenly your people talk. They are a disgrace to your good name.* Then the Noble asked one final question: "Why do you all not have stakes?"

After father and son stared at one another, the son answered, "The stakes are for killing evil Nobles like you. We have no need for them against Lord Mayerling. So we only keep one on hand." As the boy started forward, the heavy thunder of footsteps drew nearer from down the road.

It was the villagers answering the siren. In the blink of an eye, twenty or so men and women surrounded Greylancer. There would be more coming. All of them had come armed, the hatchets and lances gleaming in their hands.

A leather-vested man, who appeared to be the leader, shouted, "Prepare to die! Lord knows why you can walk about during the day, but from the looks of you, you're a Noble to be sure. Which parts are you from?"

"The North."

"North? Then you're from Greylancer's sector?" His voice fell. Even in a land safeguarded by an iron ruler, the name of the Northern Frontier's overseer was capable of rousing fear in humans.

Would they fall silent or stir in excitement upon hearing the name again? Beneath the light of day, the Noble proclaimed, "I am Greylancer."

The humans chose silence, as if they feared the light.

2

Then they heard the sound of footsteps, like a moving mountain.

The hulking shadow came toward them, each footfall shaking the ground like aftershocks.

The humans gazed up toward the heavens.

Stopping in front of the family cowering in front of their home, Greylancer wrapped an arm around the girl's waist.

Snatched up into his embrace as she was, the girl let out not a sound. Hearing his name had stunned her into a state of shock.

One of the villagers let out a doleful moan.

"Close your eyes," the Noble whispered in a strangely gentle voice.

A massive hand brushed over the girl's eyes, which had been held open by sheer terror.

Oh, light, what evil is this, so threatening in your presence? The humans succumbed to the darkness.

When they opened their eyes and uncovered their ears, they watched the girl leaning her cheek inside the Greater Noble's cape.

She seemed asleep. A look of peace, a trusting smile. Sweet dreams.

Greylancer set her down gently, like a father would a beloved child. The girl's feet alighted softly on the ground.

The girl stood on her own feet.

And still she slept.

Her pale complexion, the glossy lips. Red veins that an ambitious artist would beg to immortalize on canvas.

Wait.

Does she breathe?

By the time the question entered the villager's minds, the girl had crumpled to the ground.

The villagers looked down, riveted by the two bite marks on the girl's neck.

"You have my gratitude," said Greylancer to the girl's family. "Now I shall go and destroy Mayerling."

The name of their lord incited a reaction.

Violent emotion filled their dumbstruck faces. The girl's mother cried out first.

Then the girl's father and brother let out a scream and lunged at the Noble.

Lightning flashed across their necks.

The two heads, sailing through the air, appeared as if they were propelled by great gushes of blood.

When the heads rolled to the ground, the mob converged at once and descended upon the enemy.

Greylancer also began his advance, whirling his silver lance as he pushed forward into the crowd.

He took one steady step after the next.

One by one, the villagers fell before him and to the right and left and behind him, as their necks spouted blood like a champagne shower.

This was a Noble.

This was Greylancer.

Spattered from head to toe in blood, the giant licked the gore from his arms.

But Greylancer was growing restless.

No matter how many he felled, more humans attacked.

The fright on their faces was palpable. They were the looks of the vanquished intuiting their own defeat. Closing their eyes and gritting their teeth, nevertheless, they continued their attack, brandishing their stakes and shooting their rifles.

Why? Why do they not fear death when they will surely die? Greylancer furrowed his brows.

More footsteps. The sound of reinforcements.

But should his advance against the humans' defensive stand continue, the entire village was liable to perish.

The smell of blood filled the winter morning.

"Stop, stand back!" shouted a voice, along with the sound of horseshoes clopping in the distance. The sound grew louder until the mob parted before Greylancer, and three armored riders on black horses appeared. "We are with Lord Mayerling's patrol unit.

Are you Lord Greylancer?" the giant on the lead horse asked.

"I am."

"Ah, so you are. Please forgive the people of this village."

The three patrolmen dismounted their horses.

"They were merely acting out of devotion," said Greylancer. "Mayerling is a ruler to be envied."

"Such gracious words. We have orders to ensure your safe arrival at the castle. This way, please." The patrolman raised his hand, and a blue shuttlecraft descended from the sky and hovered three meters overhead.

"That won't be necessary. My chariot awaits." Greylancer pointed behind him. He shook his entire blood-stained body in one vicious motion, and for a moment, he disappeared in a crimson haze. When the haze dissipated, the Noble and his cape were utterly free of blood.

"You are exactly as his lordship described. Then allow us to accompany you to the castle."

"No need."

"That would leave us delinquent in our duties. We have orders not to leave your side, if we should happen upon your audience."

Thinking better of his refusal, Greylancer said, "Come," and began walking. The path underfoot was muddy. The clay caked on his boots was red.

"Lord Greylancer is a guest of Lord Mayerling. Any impertinence will not be tolerated," the patrolman announced.

The villagers were struck motionless even before the patrolman's warning. So ferocious was Greylancer in battle and so sudden the end that they had lost the will to fight.

Soon the lavish shuttlecraft and the much smaller, but elegantly adorned, chariot blazed a path to the hills south of the village and landed beyond the walls of Mayerling's impregnable castle two minutes later.

†

Despite the modest sculptures and furnishings, the choice and skillful placement of jewels and metal adornments reflected Mayerling's taste, integrity, and fortitude in such a way that a guest—even an enemy—might feel at ease. Such was the drawing room where Greylancer confronted Mayerling's coffin.

While such a meeting might appear eerie and impolite to humans, to a Noble consigned to sleeping in his coffin during the day, receiving a guest in this defenseless, vulnerable state, albeit from within a well-fortified coffin, was the highest form of hospitality.

"I've been expecting you, Lord Greylancer."

"So it seems. How did you come to learn that I walk during the day?"

"There isn't a Noble in the Frontier that doesn't know. I'm surprised the Privy Council hasn't twisted your arm to tell them your secret."

"They have."

"So they have." The voice inside the coffin let out a low laugh, imagining the outcome of the exchange. "And?"

"Virgilius was chancellor then. I pretended to lose my footing and knocked him with this lance, and he never asked of it again. After five attempted break-ins and an attack on my sister, my secret is still safe."

"Oh? How did you accomplish that?"

"Any uninvited guest that dared enter never left. As for the poor soul that attacked my sister, he fell victim to a more formidable enemy than I. The questions and summonses ceased after that."

"I hear Chancellor Virgilius never regained the use of his arm." And then, the voice, brightening with curiosity, said, "Perhaps the lands to the east, outside Noble rule, have some method of accomplishing this magical feat of yours?"

"I've heard likewise, but nothing more."

"Would you care for a smoke?"

At Mayerling's prompting, Greylancer cast a glance at the gold cigar box on the marble table. "No," he answered.

"We tried using the energy source from one of the OSB's energy emitters to aid plant growth. You may find it to your liking."

"It's a cancer risk," Greylancer said, either in jest or sarcasm. The Nobility were not in the least affected by radiation exposure.

Nevertheless, Greylancer took a cigar out of the box with some interest and cut the end with a cutter.

Lighting the end with a lighter from the table, he took a long drag and let out a swirl of blue smoke.

He lifted another cigar out of the box and said, "Quite good. And the radiation produces this?"

"Radiation discovered in the OSB's star system. It may have many uses."

Greylancer took another drag and said, "Well now—"

"You desire a duel."

"Tell me about Chancellor Cornelius first. There is a plot, I hear. Any truth to the rumor?"

"Yes, I heard it from the chancellor himself, though I doubt he'll ever speak of it again."

"Who else is involved?"

"To my knowledge, every last member of the Privy Council."

Greylancer flashed a bitter smile. "Fascinating. It appears the odds are stacked against you."

"I'm not so naïve as to choose a castle defense in a battle that I intend to lose."

"Yes, I am quite aware. My duty is to prove just that and to dash that dream. Duchess Mircalla—I should say, the supreme commander—"

"I hear the woman is quite the tactician."

"Against men as well."

"Have you been prey to her advances?" Mayerling asked, his tone dropping low.

"Not as of yet. But Macula has been 'bitten.'"

"Zeus?"

"He's always had a weakness for beautiful women. But I suspect Mircalla is not the only prize he is after."

"What is Zeus plotting? He can't be…?"

"I do not know. It's something I sensed when last we met in this very castle. Merely a hunch. I can't say for certain."

"The probability?"

"About thirty percent."

"I'll trust those odds."

"Damn if you aren't a bore to talk to." Greylancer raised his right hand, wherein the silver lance awaited its bloodbath. "Fortune be with you."

The lance pierced through the coffin and into the floor.

It took all of two breaths for the blood spilled forth from the gash in the coffin to stain the floor.

Greylancer's lips curled into a grin.

He swung the lance in an arc, heaving the coffin effortlessly through the air.

Wood, it was not. The stone coffin weighed several hundred kilograms. It smashed against the wall thirty meters away with a deafening crash and fell to the floor. Neither the wall nor floor was damaged.

"Your guest departs!" Greylancer bellowed toward the door some distance away.

†

Greylancer was summoned to the operations room at the counterinsurgency's headquarters as soon as Mircalla awakened.

"I've read the records." The fair-skinned beauty stared at Greylancer with a look that was neither disapproving nor cordial. The counterinsurgency base camp was equipped with a surveillance system in case of enemy attack. "I cannot maintain discipline when my subcommander acts alone and without notice."

"You are entirely right." Greylancer nodded, contrite. At

minimum, the law must be observed. This much was in his blood.

"So?" Mircalla asked, frigid.

"I paid a visit to Mayerling's castle and impaled him as he slept inside his coffin."

"Oh?" Her crimson lips rounded into an O, but her eyes, shaped like arrowheads, were bereft of emotion. "That much I believe. What surprises me is your safe return after killing the castle's lord."

"Then you do not know Mayerling. He left orders to treat an invited guest as a guest to the last, regardless of his own fate. His orders are inviolable."

"Then it appears this battle is over."

"Wishful thinking, I'm afraid," he said, hiding none of the contempt for the woman's shallowness. "If there is even one vassal of mettle in that castle, he will defend the castle to the last man, even after his lord has perished, and for certain if Mayerling ordered his men to resist to the last."

"According to your characterization of him, Mayerling doesn't seem the kind of Noble to give such an order."

"*If* there is a vassal of any mettle. On the other hand, they might agree to a bloodless surrender if so ordered by Mayerling. Therein lies the gamble."

"Hmm, we've been appealing for the castle's surrender, but we have yet to hear a response. Let us discuss a course of action at the war council meeting. But say nothing of our meeting here."

Greylancer grinned again, this time in admiration. *A shrewd move.*

In the event the enemy refused to surrender, and it became known that Mayerling was dead, the morale of the counterinsurgency forces would increase tenfold. Meanwhile the enemy's morale would typically decrease; however, in Mayerling's case, the veneration his vassals held for their lord was far more powerful than even a Noble's true death. Should the two armies come to blows, the counterinsurgency would face a surprisingly intractable enemy, killing its will to fight. As commander, Mircalla could ill afford to engage in a long, unnecessary battle.

†

As a result of the war council meeting, the generals, fuming from the morning's attack, had reached a consensus. They would commence the siege as soon as the barrier was neutralized.

"But our neutralizer will not work against Mayerling's barrier."

When one man voiced this reality, another said, "We have no choice but to wait until the science corps make the necessary enhancements to the neutralizer. And so, we must bide our time."

"There is no other way."

"Agreed, agreed."

A malaise filled the war room.

On the battlefield, the warriors gathered here would burn in pursuit of the enemy. But once war-making was understood as a futile exercise, the blood pulsing through their bodies turned cold, their vitality quelled. For better or for worse, this was the Noble's nature. Perhaps it was also the cause of the Nobility's eventual decline. They were ignorant of Greylancer's breach of enemy lines and murder of Mayerling. Commander Mircalla had kept the facts from even the top generals.

Greylancer, who'd closed his eyes and relegated himself to bystander, suddenly, angrily, popped his eyes open. So insufferable was the air of indecision that he had reached the end of his rope.

Would he press to ride his chariot once more and lead the attack on the enemy? Or would he defy Mircalla's intentions and tell them that Mayerling had perished?

Like fish noticing boiling magma spouting out of murky waters, the warriors turned in Greylancer's direction.

At least, they attempted to until—

A fist came crashing down atop the table.

"Lord Greylancer." The young Duke of Krolock from the Southern Frontier sector turned his flaming eyes from his trembling fist up to the great warrior. His given name was Darshan. "Never mind the others. But how can you sink into this morass of cowardice? This is intolerable! I won't stand for it! One barrier, and you're fit to sit idly by, staring off into enemy territory instead of marching upon it—and you call yourself a warrior? Commander Mircalla, if you intend to attack the castle, I beseech you, give the order now."

"And if I do, what do you propose to do?" Mircalla asked. Despite her frigid tone, she looked upon the young Noble with kindness.

"As impregnable as the barrier may be, it cannot stretch ten kilometers under the surface. Perhaps the commander is aware of the House of Krolock's renown for our subterranean attacks."

"Yes, I've seen it with my own eyes from your father. The underground mole, code name Landross."

"Indeed, we have a weapon by that name. The temperature of the magma immediately under the earth's crust in this part of the world is approximately a thousand degrees. My men will move through the magma at will, advance below Mayerling's castle, and break through from below. I beseech you to grant my men that honor."

"Denied," answered Mircalla. At this, Greylancer felt his temples twitch. She continued, "The decisions made by the war council are ironclad. No one shall disobey. Besides which, the enemy will not give in to brute force. So long as I am supreme commander, no one shall die in vain."

The young general's entire body trembled with anger. His youth struggled to forgive the vagaries of battle.

"The commander's orders." The men's eyes shot back to Greylancer as the giant stood from his chair. With the gazes of the generals gathered on him, he strode toward Darshan Krolock and rested a hand on his shoulder. "We are forbidden to defy them even in death. But in the very least, there is one true warrior in our midst. Commander, I yearn to depart for my nightly patrol."

"This concludes the war council." Mircalla's icy voice settled in the spines of the generals.

†

Beneath the moonlight, the silver-blue exteriors of the steel moles seemed to shiver in want of returning underground.

The hulking vehicles, measuring a hundred meters long, were capable of twisting themselves through the ground like enormous insects, albeit ones with conical drills instead of mandibles and caterpillar belts instead of six legs.

Soldiers were standing at attention next to the ten moles.

They were about to deploy a forbidden assault from a barrier-protected area of the camp that would allow them to elude detection. The eyes of the soldiers shone crimson, and their white fangs gleamed in the shadows cast by their helmets.

Standing before the men already briefed of their mission and awaiting their command, Darshan Krolock, himself outfitted in battle gear, quietly pointed at the steel insects. "Board your vehicles."

The men ran without a sound.

As Krolock moved to follow, a rust-tinged voice called out from behind, "Do you go?"

"Lord Greylancer." The eyes of the young leader were filled with reverence. "You knew?"

"No." Greylancer shook his head. "It was only that I would do the same."

"I beg of you to overlook what you've seen here."

"It appears the sodden air of the war council has done something to my eyes." Greylancer affected a bleary-eyed look. "We possess the technology to manufacture drill-shaped tanks with liquid metals, yet we cannot escape the old," he said, referring to the crude build of the subterranean vehicle. By all appearances, it was beyond outdated—rather like an ancient toy weapon out of a magazine from eons ago. The body was even held together with steel rivets. "Perhaps the height of the Nobility's fondness for anachronism. I shall not stop you, but will you not reconsider?"

"I'm surprised you would ask. The battle is decided in life and death. I can no longer stand idly by on the battlefield in uncertainty." Krolock rolled up his sleeves and said, "Just you see, Lord Greylancer. If we cannot breach the castle from underground and capture Mayerling, we shall destroy his castle. Even if we must undermine its foundations and sink it into the mantle layer." The young Noble smiled an invincible smile.

Greylancer looked on silently as the steel moles burrowed, one after the next, into the earth. The roar of the machines was stifled by the earth itself as they pushed under the surface. "A dreadful thing," he muttered to himself.

Overhearing this, a white-haired officer who happened nearby asked, "How do you mean?"

Greylancer's answer was immediate. "That such a young Noble must perish before the likes of you."

CHAPTER 9:
CONSPIRATORIAL
PURGATORY

1

The counterinsurgency camp was shrouded in tension.

A senior officer in Krolock's unit had reported the young general's covert attack to Mircalla.

"They will be disciplined upon their return," Mircalla answered as if she'd predicted it all along. Then she informed her top brass.

It would have been only natural for the fifty unit commanders to storm into headquarters in a fit of rage.

However, when only two officers had come to register complaints, Greylancer let slip a bitter smile. "So our morality has slackened to this."

Mircalla smiled. "I pray it is only our morality."

"What else—"

"Our souls." Mircalla laid a hand on her generous bosom. "Would you mind if I sighed?"

"It doesn't suit you."

Mircalla waved her hand in the air instead.

An aerial schematic of Mayerling's castle appeared.

"Such an elegant castle," said Mircalla, making no secret of her admiration.

"Indeed. Noble castles have typically been rustic. However, everything about House Mayerling is unconventional."

"And what do you make of that?"

"Make, Commander?"

"It is an act of defiance against the Nobility. Vlijmen Mayerling's father, Ryan Mayerling—he, too, was a nonconformist. A human sympathizer. He began this travesty of abolishing every tribute but one, demanding only a blood tithe, which he did not drink directly from humans himself."

"I am aware."

"Then are you aware of the Privy Council's plot, Lord Greylancer?"

"I have heard whispers, yes."

"If they are allowed to liberate even the Frontier, this world will essentially fall into the hands of the Privy Council. You and I both know, the Sacred Ancestor entrusted us with overseeing the Frontier fearing this very outcome. We must carry out his will if this planet falls to ruin. Why would Chancellor Cornelius covet control over the Frontier, rather than the world, at the expense of the Sacred Ancestor's will? And so suddenly?"

"Why indeed," answered Greylancer, even as he wondered just what Mircalla and Zeus were plotting. He felt a smile escape his lips. The Noble was not averse to intrigue. In fact, if overseeing the Frontier had taught him anything, it was that chicanery was part of the Nobles' natural disposition. "Commander Mircalla," said Greylancer. "What is Zeus—"

"Commander," interrupted a mechanized voice.

"What is it?" asked Mircalla blankly.

"We detected ten explosions two thousand meters below ground." The voice reported the coordinates and continued, "It is thought to be the location of Lord Krolock's Landross." Mircalla closed her eyes, while Greylancer let out a sigh. "A massive unidentified body is ascending from the explosion. It's burrowing this way. At its current course, it will surface in the middle of Lord Greylancer's encampment at 19:19."

Greylancer cocked his head down at the gold badge on the collar of his cape. "This is Greylancer. Inform the men to fall back ten kilometers east within four minutes. Transfer weapons and provisions by 19:18. But if it cannot be done, abandon all equipment."

Mircalla directed her wan countenance toward her second in command. Try as she might, the duchess could not hide her shock. "A Noble the likes of Greylancer giving an order to abandon weapons and flee? Do my eyes deceive me?"

"I am not entirely certain myself," he answered morosely. "Commander, you should get yourself to safety immediately. Whatever this thing is will surface in the midst of our troops, but it may still be capable of laying waste to the entire army."

"Yes, I am aware." Mircalla rose to her feet with a grace that would elicit any watcher's sighs.

Within three minutes, the army had retreated to its designated position.

The earth ruptured, and the gargantuan ground dweller revealed itself before the eyes of the terrestrial world.

Whether its morphology was suited to surviving underground was questionable.

When the creature emerged fully from the ground, it stood two hundred meters tall and three hundred meters long, with plates made of bedrock covering its beetle-shaped body. An avalanche of dirt and gravel spilled down from between its densely packed plates, snapping the trees below like toothpicks. The two protuberances on the sides of its head appeared to be eyes that had atrophied from disuse. The prolegs lining the ventral part of the abdomen gripped the ground.

General Yunus, Greylancer's second in command, had pulled back the barrier along with his men, so that it cornered the creature against Mayerling's barrier behind it.

The creature charged forward, as was its instinct, crashed against the barrier shielding the Greylancer forces, and was repelled back. Rather than maneuver laterally, which was clear of obstacles, it continued to face off against the invisible wall.

A white mist began to emanate from the creature's flanks.

"What is that?" asked Mircalla from the newly transferred headquarters.

"Those rocky plates on its exoskeleton are no ordinary scales,"

Greylancer answered. "They're likely vibrating plates for moving through the earth. If I'm right, this is about to get interesting." The Noble let slip a grin.

"I fail to see the humor in this."

Before Mircalla had scarcely finished, a mechanized voice reported, "Commander, our barrier is weakening!"

Stunned, Mircalla let out, "No! Can the creature be...?"

"It's emitting an oscillatory wave used to crush gravel and rock as it burrows through the earth. It might be more powerful than the gravitational barrier can bear," explained Greylancer, amused. This unfamiliar creature was a precious plaything that made the warrrior's heart dance with excitement. "When the barrier is destroyed, deploy air chariots. Attack the creature from behind."

"From behind?" Mircalla asked.

"Yes." The Noble's eyes gleamed. "The barrier is weakening." He eyed the holographic screen projected in the air, where the creature charged the invisible barrier again, broke through, and scuttled toward the Greylancer forces deployed before it.

Air chariots shot into the air as if to escape but quickly circled back and dropped several black objects at the moving target's abdomen.

A dimensional corrosion bomb hit one of the rock plates and opened a hole about ten meters in diameter, which grew gradually larger.

The bomb was designed to rend a hole in the dimension and drag its target into another dimension. No monster had the means to escape it.

"It's glowing again," said Mircalla, to which Greylancer nodded.

The creature was wrapped in a dazzling white light. After a moment when the glow dissipated, the gaping hole in the creature's abdomen had stopped expanding.

The oscillation wave had halted the dimensional corrosion.

"This thing is too dangerous," said Mircalla, shaking her head.

"Wait."

As if prompted by Greylancer's voice, the massive creature,

weighing perhaps tens, if not hundreds of thousands of tons, spun 180 degrees in the other direction.

Mayerling's barrier now loomed before it. The creature began to glow again.

"Look, not even Mayerling's barrier will slow it down."

With the creature's every advance, the ground sank around it, destroying buildings nearby.

This had been Greylancer's strategy all along—to attack the creature from behind to trick it into believing that the attack was Mayerling's doing and to coerce it into destroying the barrier.

"Now, Commander!"

Mircalla gave only a curt nod. "Mobilize the entire army toward the breach point!"

The army generals had already been briefed in the event of a full-scale offensive.

Beneath the moonlight, the counterinsurgency forces commenced their advance.

Mircalla blinked her eyes in astonishment.

A single chariot shot into the sky over Mayerling's dominion as if in want of the first strike. Just who was—?

Mircalla glanced to her right.

Her second in command had vanished.

†

Bathed in moonlight, Greylancer raced the air chariot toward Castle Mayerling.

The wind lashed his face like a sea of whips. The Noble had no use for a barrier. Clashing against the elements headfirst was how Greylancer took the fight to the enemy.

He made visual confirmation of Castle Mayerling. No anti-aircraft fire or intercepting vessels. Even as he suspected a trap, Greylancer thought, *The Devil may care, but I alone shall be the one to perish.*

"Full ahead!"

No sooner had he shouted these words than Mircalla's face floated up before him on the chariot's monitor. "The operation has been called off, Lord Greylancer."

"What?" he blurted out.

"Mayerling's generals have officially abdicated. The battle is over. Redirect your efforts to destroying the subterranean creature.

"Mayerling's dominion is now under the control of the central government. We must eliminate any threat ravaging the territory. When that is done, you will accompany me to the surrender agreement."

"Understood."

The castle keep drew closer up ahead.

Saying nothing, Greylancer turned the chariot around and set course for the subterranean monster. The look pasted on his face had far surpassed anger; he wore an expression only of blank indignation.

2

Once a surrender agreement had been reached, the top commanders besieged Greylancer with questions.

The brunt of their censure was directed at the fact that Greylancer had killed Mayerling and concealed his death and for his daring to go against the war council's decision and act alone.

For the former violation, Mircalla explained that Greylancer had been acting on her orders. As for the latter, it was decided that Greylancer would be disciplined pending the Privy Council's deliberation.

After enduring the litany of charges against him in silence, Greylancer rose from the table, shot a vicious look that nearly drained blood from the faces of the self-satisfied generals, and exited the chamber. Outside, he caught up with General Berneige, a commander in Mayerling's army, as he was preparing to return to the castle.

"Where is Mayerling's tomb?" Greylancer asked.

"Oh, do you wish to lay some flowers?"

Greylancer bared his fangs. "A true warrior would take no pleasure in such a gesture from the enemy." Then he lowered his voice and said, "There is a matter I wish to look into."

"He lies in the basement altar of House Mayerling inside the castle."

"Very well. I shall be there in an hour's time. I pray the door will be open." Greylancer's eyes glinted with a look of resolve.

†

Never had the burden of war been so light on the attacking army, and never had there been a more dissatisfying end to fighting.

As fortunate an outcome a bloodless surrender was, a battle was an opportunity for warriors to win both distinction and reward. Had the castle fallen, they were also free to plunder its spoils. Since time immemorial, it was an unwritten law of war.

Yet this engagement had provided no such opportunity. The enemy commander had been defeated before battle, and his surviving generals could do little more than fight back tears and their own bloodlust to honor their master's orders of an unconditional surrender of the castle.

Naturally, the generals of the counterinsurgency forces had directed their ire at Greylancer.

Plenty of past commanders who'd found themselves in the same circumstance had been assassinated. That Greylancer had not suffered the same fate was a testament to his might.

An hour later, Greylancer had set foot inside the catacombs. Aside from the chief steward ushering them inside, the Noble brought with him only one companion—not a soldier but a protégé he'd taken under his wing.

Moonlight shone down upon the spacious floor, the stone cobbled walls and extravagant coffins each taking up space in numerous depressions in the walls.

The moon, stars, and sky above were all holographic projections.

Greylancer asked the steward leading the way, "Would you say your master was a vain man?"

"Gracious, no!" The blond-haired steward shook his head. "Lord Mayerling never expressed interest in worldly acquisitions. If by chance you are referring to the coffin, his lordship was merely honoring the wishes of his father."

"So it was his old man who was vain." Greylancer tapped one of the coffins with his silver lance.

Because they were blessed with agelessness, few Nobles ever died.

Though ancestral coffins lined the catacombs after the burial methods of human noble houses, the coffins were nothing more than decoration holding not a single corpse. That Greylancer felt compelled to ask after Mayerling's vanity spoke to just how many Nobles were given to such an unnecessary practice.

"This way," said the steward at last, a bit crossly, after escorting Greylancer and his companion in silence. Stopping, he gestured toward the door ahead. "The tomb of the last head of House Mayerling."

When Greylancer opened the door, a cavernous chamber more spacious than the last spread before him. *This is no illusion*, thought the Noble.

In the center of the marble floor roughly two hundred meters ahead lay a coffin atop a bronze altar encircled by four candle stands. Orange-colored flames danced in the reflection of the surface of the coffin.

There was a scar where Greylancer's lance had pierced the lid.

"I can go no further," said the steward. "When your business is done, please see yourselves out."

Leaving the escort at the door, Greylancer and his retainer passed through the doors of the chamber.

The Noble took about fifty strides toward the altar and stopped.

Blue shadows descended from the ceiling, intercepting Greylancer's advance.

Four men and two women dressed like farmers. Given how

they had swooped down from a ceiling beam a hundred meters high, they were not human.

"Half-humans." Greylancer's eyes burned crimson. "Who alerted you to my coming?"

Their answer was an all-out attack.

The four men attacked with swords, while the two women took aim with stake guns. The half-humans had chosen not to open with a projectile attack, knowing Greylancer's lance was fast enough to strike down their bullets. They held back, waiting for an opening, as the four men charged headlong into what would certainly be their deaths.

One half-human woman aimed for Greylancer's companion standing next to his master.

But the gunpowder in the flash pan of the companion's flint-lock rifle ignited first.

A report from the woman's gun followed, sending a stake whizzing toward the target at five hundred meters per second. If neither could evade the other's bullet, they would both surely be hit.

Neither shooter had time to react.

The gunner's bullet hit the stake in midair and shattered it.

In the next instant, the gunner drew the flintlock gun from his waist and drilled a bullet between the woman's eyes.

The woman's head was thrown backward as she fell on her back, smoke smoldering from the bullet hole dead center.

The second woman aimed at the gunner next. The sharpshooter dove to the ground and rolled several times even as he took aim with a four-barreled pepperbox. A more developed weapon than the flintlock, this gun had a percussion cap.

The hammer ignited a charge. When the gun fired, however, the woman had already taken cover. The bullet missed her by meters.

Meanwhile, Greylancer, casually parrying the four swords arrayed against him, beheaded two of the men with a single swing of his lance.

The third man had leapt over the sideways swing of the lance and threatened to strike down Greylancer from above, while the fourth had ducked and now skittered on his knees toward the Noble.

Neither had expected the lance to reverse course.

Rather than continuing its sideways trajectory, the lance sprang back in the opposite direction and skewered the half-human bearing down overhead and plunged into the fourth man's back, pinning him against the floor.

Greylancer fixed an amused look on the man thrashing and screeching like an insect on the ground, and called out, "Gallagher."

"I have disposed of the rest." The gunner finished reloading his gun and rifle and rose from his knee. This man, giving Greylancer a curt nod, was none other than the gunner whom Greylancer had captured after foiling his attempt to assassinate Mayerling only several days ago. "But these are not half-humans…"

The half-human attackers, save the barrel-chested man skewered by Greylancer's lance, had melted into puddles of glowing pale blue ooze. After giving up their human hosts, the OSB had returned to their original forms.

"I detected no one, much less the likes of you, following us. You must have been waiting for us here." Greylancer twisted the lance. The OSB still keeping the form of the barrel-chested man writhed in agony. "Answer. Who told you of our coming? Why do you wish us dead?"

The man did not answer. The Noble gave his lance another twist.

"Beats…me…" the man finally sputtered. "The boss…told us…to ambush you…here…is all…" he answered in the rustic manner of a farmer. The OSB always borrowed the memories, and thus the language, of the beings it possessed.

"Who is this boss you speak of?"

Silence.

Greylancer twisted the lance.

And then a scream.

"Rafa…I…don't…zunzun…know…shiga…ri…" So unbearable was his pain that the OSB had forgotten its adopted memories, its words no longer of this world.

Its screams, too, ceased to sound human.

Do you continue to twist and plunge the lance into the victim's stomach to divine the truth, dear Greylancer? The Noble smoldered with a look of rapture, relishing the sight of the man struggling to swallow its last breaths.

"That's quite enough."

Greylancer whirled in the direction of the voice. He had not sensed the arrival of a new presence. Gallagher remained down on one knee and jerked his rifle up to his shoulder, shaken.

"What brings you here, Chancellor Cornelius?" Greylancer asked coolly. The figure in white robes and dark gown standing before him was indeed the bearer of that name. Since the councilors had not taken part in the counterinsurgency, the chancellor's presence confirmed Greylancer's suspicions. "So you are behind this intrigue."

"Sadly, no. There is another," answered the old chancellor as he untied the strings of his gown. "My part is to drive the stake that will send you to your death."

"I had not considered that you were capable of manipulating the OSB. I must ask—what ties do you have with the invaders?"

"The Nobility's defeat is inevitable," said Chancellor Cornelius, stone-faced.

"Odd." Greylancer arched a brow. "It is true that their science is superior to ours. However, we are in possession of a more fundamental and decisive advantage. We possess eternal life."

"Provided that a stake is not driven into our hearts," added Chancellor Cornelius. His voice spread over the chamber like a curse. "But we are also hampered by what you call a fundamental and decisive disadvantage, which the Privy Council and Ultimate Mind have pointed out will lead to our eventual downfall for hundreds of years—the degeneration of the Noble race."

A certain sound reverberated inside Greylancer's mind.

An indescribable yet certain echo of destruction.

"On the second day of the war against the OSB, the Ultimate Mind prophesied our defeat. That is to say our degeneration will be the cause of our fall three thousand years from now. Those are the words of the Sacred Ancestor himself, Lord Greylancer."

During the dawn of the Noble civilization, with which Greylancer was unfamiliar, the Sacred Ancestor had vanished, leaving behind an enormous computer to advise the Noble leaders in his place. Kept inside the inner chamber of the Privy Council Ministry, this Ultimate Mind continued to bestow the Nobility with the words of the Sacred Ancestor to this day.

Greylancer sighted a gray swirl churning before his very eyes. A chaotic vortex that threatened to swallow the hollow wills of all mortal creatures great and small. Nay, even the wills of the immortal.

"A decision handed down by the Sacred Ancestor cannot be overturned," the chancellor continued. "So we contacted the OSB through back channels and initiated negotiations. The aliens proclaimed that their interstellar conquest was the will of their god. That this conflict was about shedding a ray of civilization onto the ignorant masses whom understood nothing of their god.

"It was for this reason the OSB rejected our offer of truce, and so the war continued. But five days ago, a faction occupying a stronghold vital to the OSB conquest secretly declared their willingness to negotiate a cease fire. We reached a tentative peace agreement on the same day, one in which this planet will come under OSB rule."

"That's absurd!" The warrior's cry thundered across the corners of the chamber.

"Exactly right. The Ultimate Mind had predicted that you would utter those very words. As well as another—Mayerling."

"..."

"Of course, Mayerling knew nothing of our negotiations with the OSB. He had gotten wind of the plasma attack to exterminate the OSB enclaves and of the demand that the Frontier would be made to submit to the Privy Council's control. Had he learned the truth, Mayerling would no doubt have said and acted in much the way you have. In that sense, his subjugation in accordance with the central government's decision was a stroke of good fortune. And now, Lord Greylancer, you will follow him in death."

No sooner had he said the word *death* than Chancellor Cornelius's head detached from his body and shot up in the air. Kicking off the ground, the rest of his body followed.

Greylancer took aim and plunged his lance past the old man's flowing robes and into his headless body.

3

The chancellor's body reunited with his head some twenty meters in the air, despite the lance piercing clear through the chest.

Chancellor Cornelius smiled. "Do what you will, Lord Greylancer. This body is nothing more than an illusion with physical substance, which is why you do not see me submerged in my usual eutrophic fluid. Your lance is useless against me. *This*, on the other hand—" Sticking a hand in a pocket of his robe, the chancellor produced a small glass bottle.

A shot rang out. The bullet blew off the chancellor's wrinkled hand holding the glass bottle, sending it skittering across the floor.

"Well now, this is a skilled servant," said the chancellor, glancing at Gallagher with his rifle at the ready. "Alas, such shallow wit. Did you not see that the glass bottle was real? Now you shall go to hell, smelling the pleasant scent contained within."

Greylancer felt his knees go weak. He crumpled to the ground, losing his grip on his lance. A sweet nectarlike scent began to fill the cavernous space. The scent brought down even the half-human Gallagher.

The liquid that had been sealed inside the bottle emitted the sweetest, most evil scent. One that would cause any Noble to fall into a stupor.

"Now then." Chancellor Cornelius righted himself and, after withdrawing the lance tip from his chest, sidled next to where Greylancer lay. The chancellor, of course, was but an illusion.

He took out a white wooden stake and hammer from his pockets. Having physical substance, he was capable of handling solid objects.

The old man pressed the stake against Greylancer's heart and raised the hammer high over his head. A spike driven into the heart would surely send a Noble, even Greylancer, to his death. Who would have guessed that such a mighty warrior would meet his end in this way?

No doubt Greylancer was as amazed. He was still conscious. It was his body that could not move. One Greater Noble would soon vanish from this moonlit world.

The chancellor brought down the hammer with all his might and suddenly stopped in mid-swing. With an elegance defying his wizened face, the old man leapt five meters and landed in a low crouch, shooting a suspicious look at the stone coffin resting on the bronze altar.

Stone grinding against stone, slowly the heavy lid of the coffin slid back.

The lavish sarcophagus was supposed to contain only Mayerling's mortal remains.

But surely a corpse turned to dust had no hands with which to grip the sides of the coffin, nor a body to raise to a sitting position. The shadowy figure alighted from the coffin and fixed its gray eyes on the old Noble.

"Mayerling?" shouted Cornelius in disbelief.

"Regretfully no," answered the man. "I am Shizam, a swordsman only recently serving under Lord Mayerling. It is an honor, Chancellor Cornelius."

"How dare you appear before me, human! Begone!"

"That will not do, I'm afraid. My master has tasked me with protecting the Noble Greylancer," said the swordsman, glancing down at the warrior struggling still to regain his senses.

There was a sound of steel rattling against steel as Shizam gripped the hilts of the two swords strapped behind his back and lunged. The illusory Cornelius produced a sword of his own. *Clang! Clang!* the swords rang out.

"The sound of your sword betrays your skill," said the swordsman. "Best you leave your head at my feet."

"Shizam, was it? Just how do you propose to behead this illusion before you?"

The swordsman answered quietly, "Streda..."

"No!" Cornelius flinched. "You practice—" The old Noble leapt back and hurled a stake. The second flash of steel—the sword in Shizam's left hand—struck down the projectile.

Chancellor Cornelius landed on his feet and threw back his head. Actually, his head fell away entirely. The first flash of steel—the sword in Shizam's right hand—had sliced across Cornelius's neck before Cornelius could even see the blade.

While the fall echoed across the cavernous chamber, Shizam plunged his sword into the old Noble's heart.

After watching the man's body swirl and dissolve into thin air, like paint mixing into water, Shizam ran to Greylancer's side.

"Are you all right?"

"I will live...The effects of the evil incense is wearing off."

"I am glad you will recover."

"What has happened to Chancellor Cornelius?"

"The Chancellor has met his doom," answered Shizam.

"But the man before you was an illusion."

"I possess the Streda skill."

Greylancer arched a brow. "I have heard of this skill developed to kill Nobles. Is it effective against apparitions?"

"Yes. The moment I struck down his apparition, his physical form—wherever it might have been—also took its last breath." Shizam answered quietly, though with no small hint of pride. Suddenly, he felt two icy daggers penetrate his body.

Still lying on his side, Greylancer stared at the swordsman. "Perhaps you wish to match swords with this Noble." When Shizam did not answer, he growled, "Speak."

Even in this circumstance, nay *any* circumstance, Shizam was never one to refuse a duel. Take on all comers—it was the cardinal rule of swordsmen.

Seconds passed before he finally answered, "I accept."

"Never mind," said Greylancer, shaking his head. "You have already lost the battle of wills. Damn that Mayerling. Why did he order you inside the coffin? Surely he did not harbor a vendetta against me."

"That I do not know. Only that he was sure you would come and that I was to come to your aid if something should go awry."

"Awry indeed. What did you know, Mayerling?" Greylancer jumped to his feet like a spring-action toy and approached Gallagher, who was also beginning to stir. He commanded, "After me," and strode toward the way out of the catacombs.

Watching the gunner writhing as he struggled against the effects of the evil incense, Shizam let out a sigh and with heavy steps went to Gallagher's aid.

†

Leaving the troop withdrawal to Yunus and the others, Greylancer rushed back to the Capital with the gunner Gallagher in tow.

The western sky rippled with the last traces of daylight. The Noble night was just beginning.

Greylancer hurried directly home.

Though the blinds and shutters were shut, a faint light pervaded the mansion. The property was not shrouded in complete darkness. This was another peculiar Noble custom. Aside from their coffins, the Nobility did not demand absolute darkness from the rest of the world.

Many, like Mayerling, elected to recreate night by simulating the moon and stars.

"Laria!" Greylancer shouted upon entering the parlor.

Three shadows appeared. They were guardroids tasked with protecting their masters while the vampires slept in the light of day.

"Is something the matter?" asked the humanoid steward, to which Greylancer replied with a swing of his lance.

The steward and the guardroids were sent hurtling across the room where they crashed in a pile, sparks flying until they fell motionless.

"Clear the way, worthless machines."

Greylancer headed for the grand staircase, whereupon a voice called down, "Didn't anyone teach you that a warrior must always keep his wits about him?" Atop the gently curving staircase stood Laria, wearing a turquoise gown.

"You wear it too, Laria?" he asked, referring to the time-deceiving incense. Laria had invented it.

"Courtesy is golden even with whom we are most familiar. Silence is golden even at home. Isn't that so, Brother?"

"I have something I must ask." Greylancer kicked the ground. The sight of the giant easily weighing a hundred kilograms lofting upward might have even been called beautiful.

When he landed at the top of the staircase, however, Laria was on her way down. Taking the stairs one step at a time, she appeared to glide down in one fluid motion. "You dare mock your brother?" Greylancer jumped over the railing after her and landed at the foot of the staircase.

Brother and sister faced off in the center of the parlor like mortal enemies.

"I was very nearly turned to ash at Mayerling's castle. I smelled something—a familiar fragrance similar to the time-deceiving incense."

Laria's face turned ashen. "How can…Brother, are you certain?"

"No questions, Laria. The answer I seek is simple. Who else is in possession of the time-deceiving incense?"

As might be expected of the sister of the Noble Greylancer, Laria quickly regained her wits. "Varossa…he'd asked to make some enhancements to it."

CHAPTER 10:
THE FIERY CHARIOT

1

Even after noticing Greylancer enter the marble dome, Varossa did not falter from the task at hand. Whenever he was engrossed in his work, the eccentric weaponsmith was prone to forget not only his master's visage and name, but also his severe disposition.

Varossa dipped an iron ladle into a massive cauldron and examined the molten steel contained within it. "Damn it!" He dipped into the cauldron again and scooped up another spoonful. This time he nodded, muttered, "Good," poured the orange liquid into a trough, and watched it ooze ten meters into a small tank below. "Well now." Satisfied, the old man removed the heat-resistant goggles from his face and began to descend the stairs toward Greylancer.

Swirls of smoke rose up from his asbestos vest and gloves.

Removing his gloves, Varossa came down the flight of stairs and started at the sight of his master standing but an arm's length away. "My lord, when did you return?"

"Just now, on urgent business."

"Is that so," muttered Varossa indifferently. "Might your business be with me?"

"That is why I've come. You know about the time-deceiving incense?"

"Why of course. Miss Laria's idea was a stroke of pure genius—albeit the idea alone was hers."

"You were in possession of its formula during a period of five days about six months ago. Did you give anyone the incense or its formula during those five days?"

Varossa blinked twice before the question registered in his mind. "Did *I*, you ask?"

"Yes."

"To anyone?"

"Yes."

"Miss Laria's invention?"

"That's right."

"On my life. No one."

"Will you swear by the Sacred Ancestor?"

"Yes, by the Sacred Ancestor." Then Varossa tilted his head upward in an affected manner and said, "Now, wait a minute…"

Seeing this, Greylancer continued, "Very well. Can you think of anyone who might have had access to the incense during the five days it was in your possession?" The air around them seemed to turn crimson under the glow of Greylancer's eyes. "Varossa?" urged Greylancer.

"I cannot say."

"Hmm. You are aware of the penalty for your answer?"

"My lord, I should like to take leave of my duties. I pray there will be no error in the payment of my wages. There were two such errors in my five thousand years of service, though I overlooked the slights in the past."

"Fine. Go where you will. But after my business is done." Greylancer took a step forward.

Varossa reached into his coat pocket and scattered something on the floor. What it was exactly was indiscernible.

A brick wall about five meters square burst forth from the ground and shot up between the men.

"Any fool can conjure a steel compression wall. But a brick wall took a bit of work." Varossa watched the wall disintegrate before his very eyes. "Alas, brick is not terribly effective."

"Do not fool with me, Varossa." Greylancer drew back his lance.

The weaponsmith threw down another object at his master's feet.

This time, a stone wall shot up from the ground. The center slid open, revealing a stone corridor.

"Come inside," Varossa's voice echoed from within.

One swing of Greylancer's lance was capable of destroying such a contrivance.

Yet the warrior remained motionless, his lance lowered at his side.

Varossa was using him as a guinea pig for his latest invention—that much was clear. But Greylancer kept his temper in check, knowing that this longtime weaponsmith was burning with desperation, risking life and death at this very moment.

"Enter, my lord," the voice said, more a command than request.

Greylancer's eyes glowed blood red. The Noble entered the corridor, leaving behind the burning afterglow of his eyes.

Varossa waited for him ten meters ahead, a mere ten paces away by Greylancer's gait.

When he was but a step away from where Varossa stood, a stone wall shot up before him. No, it was Greylancer that had turned a corner. Yet he had experienced the sensation of walking in a straight line toward his prey. Varossa stood and waited ten meters ahead, as before.

"A maze," muttered Greylancer, seeing through the trick. If the contrivance were set at an entrance, any intruder would wander for an eternity inside an endless labyrinth.

But this was no time to admire the weaponsmith's handiwork.

The Noble warrior unleashed the might of his lance upon the rock faces on either side of him.

The walls came crumbling down with one blow. Greylancer stepped over the smoky rubble and stopped before Varossa. "A decent contraption, but it suffers from your personal taste. You need only make the walls sturdier."

"I'm delighted by your most tedious remarks," Varossa said, bowing slightly. When he raised his downcast eyes, the silver tip of the lance was pointed at his nose. The weaponsmith shuddered. "I cannot reveal the name, my lord. You will have to strike me dead."

Greylancer muttered, "Very well," and drove the blade through the weaponsmith's throat.

†

Upon his return, Greylancer found Laria waiting for him at the mansion.

"What are you doing?" he asked his younger sister. "Go get some rest."

"I can't help but feel something terrible is about to happen. Was it cloudy outside?"

"When I first arrived, yes."

He knew not what the weather had to do with Laria's premonition.

The comm on his collar vibrated, and a hologram of the gunner Gallagher floated up before him. Greylancer had tasked him with watching over the central government.

"My lord, about two thousand androsoldiers have departed the Capital and are headed in your direction."

"Are you certain?"

"Yes."

"Stand by." With a wave of his hand, Greylancer brought up an exterior image of the mansion.

Black dots appeared in the sky lit with the first rays of dawn, grew larger, and resolved into black aircraft. The small fleet descended and landed around House Greylancer. Equipped with magnetic propulsion systems, none of the missile-shaped aircraft needed stabilizing wings.

"They came prepared. Armed to the teeth with nuclear missiles. It speaks highly of your reputation, Brother," Laria said, her voice free of anything but sincere admiration.

Upon a Noble's capture, his land and property were con-fiscated. In much the same way, his treasure, jewels, and art, as well as all arms and inventions, became the property of the central government.

Where Greylancer was concerned, however, the government's plan was to vaporize House Greylancer whole. The central govern-ment knew full well that they were dealing with someone who knew not the word for surrender.

When the androsoldiers had taken their positions outside the mansion, a robotic voice blared forth. "Lord Greylancer, we are with the Investigation Bureau's 25th AS Combat Police Unit. You are a suspect in the murder of the chancellor of the Privy Council. You will return with us to the Capital."

"And if I refuse?"

"Forgive us, we have been empowered to take exceptional mea-sures. We will have no choice but to proceed to the nuclear option."

"Do what you must, but I shall be forced to retaliate."

"We will count to ten. If you do not surrender, we will respond with necessary force."

"Suit yourself," scoffed Greylancer.

The voice of the androsoldier rang across the mansion. "Ten. Nine. Eight…"

"Now what, Laria?"

"What ever shall we do now, Brother?" Greylancer exchanged a rare, invincible smile with his sister.

Exactly ten seconds later, the Greylancer property was engulfed in white-hot flames.

A tight gravitational shield was spread over the property, so the conflagration was contained within the grounds, thereby affecting none of the outlying areas.

†

Satisfied by the news of Greylancer's destruction, members of the central government and Privy Council lay awake inside their coffins and contemplated how they might appease the many supporters of the brave warrior in the Capital.

"A bit of a pity, really." Zeus Macula gazed at the scorched rubble and the bowl-shaped crater in the earth on the aerial screen and emptied his glass in one gulp. The glass had contained the blood of a farmer girl who'd wandered in earlier that day. Zeus was in Mircalla's private residence in the Southern Frontier sector's regional capital of Salazar. "I would rather have revealed the truth before sending Greylancer to his death. Alas, it was not meant to be. He will never return to this world, irradiated and banished to another dimension as he is. No, Greylancer shall not reconstitute physical form again."

From the depths of the moonlit space, a lyrical voice rang out, though its cadence was elegaic. "In addition to being a warrior, there was too much of the investigator in him, I'm afraid."

At the other end of the enormous table stood the ghostly figure of Duchess Mircalla. A gentle wind swayed her hair and the grass at her feet. The two overseers were in the midst of a private banquet in an illusory meadow.

"He threatened to uncover the truth far faster than either of us imagined. Time was ripe for Greylancer's curtain to fall."

"Right you are." Zeus Macula stretched and let out a long yawn. He and Mircalla had awakened from their coffins only minutes prior. Ten hours had passed since Greylancer's annihilation.

"Chancellor Cornelius's death was unfortunate, but the Privy Council has sent word of the next meeting with the OSB. We shall have to prepare terms so the OSB will grant us control over the Frontier."

"*Grant?* You must abandon such sodden thinking." Mircalla's eyes gleamed as she fixed a long look on her companion. "The OSB's reign over this planet will last for but a moment. After one or two millennia, when their power has fallen into decay, we will vanquish the enemy and regain our supremacy. To this end, waging a meaningless war that would only lead to our ruin is the height of folly. How fortunate that the Privy Council is in agreement."

"Those graybeards look upon you as their beloved. What man can resist seeing your pale flesh, hearing you whisper your desires into their ears, especially when those desires favor him?"

"The dissenters among them have been banished to some distant dimension. But they, too, might eventually come around and fall in line with the aliens." Mircalla floated next to Zeus and cupped his rugged face in her slender hands.

Meeting her advance with a look of enchantment, Zeus fought back the desire to suckle her scarlet lips with every fiber of his body, feeling her hot breath on his face only inches away. "A millennium or two—even ten millennia is but the blink of an eye."

Just as his lips brushed against hers, the duchess pulled away, like a fish carried backward by a current.

Zeus stood and moved to follow, but the eerily luminescent figure danced across the dimly lit meadow and evaded his grasp for several minutes, until finally his outstretched fingers touched her skin.

They tangled in the thick grass, letting out fevered breaths.

Beneath the pale moonlight, the duchess whispered, "Oh, Zeus. Your fangs upon my throat."

"Oh, the taste of your blood! Why? Human blood is warm, but why is Noble blood as cold as our skin?" His breath turned to moans as Mircalla sank her fangs into his neck.

"Your blood soothes me like ice water. See how it runs from my mouth down to my bosom."

Zeus pressed his lips against the swell of her chest as if the world existed only for them and began to unlace her bodice.

There was a sudden snarl of steel and a flesh-rending sound.

Zeus and Mircalla screamed.

The two writhed and tried to tear away from one another. But it was no use. Their bodies were pinned down against the illusory ground, skewered by a great lance.

When the shadow came around and hulked over them, Zeus Macula shouted, "N—Noble Greylancer!"

2

Zeus and Mircalla gaped with bloodshot eyes at the giant overshadowing them.

The intensity and unearthly aura were unmistakably those of a great warrior. But how was this possible? They had just witnessed his end via holographic projection.

"Pity that time for recreation is so fleeting."

That voice—Greylancer was alive!

His resurrection roused many questions.

To begin with, how had he managed it?

Greylancer raised his left hand.

The image of the burned ruins of the Greylancer mansion floated in the air.

Greylancer rested a hand on the top edge of the image and then shifted it down, revealing another image underneath. There stood the mansion in its unblemished splendor.

"A live image," said Greylancer. "To anyone else including the surveillance satellites, the mansion would appear to be in ruins."

"The police unit..." Zeus groaned, a hint of curiosity in his anguish. "Did they not fire their missiles?"

"That they did—into uninhabited territory. The unit erred in their target and was none the wiser for it."

Zeus and Mircalla, their mouths agape, could not speak.

"My residence remains where it has always stood, though it will appear to lie in ruins to anyone laying eyes on it."

"How?" asked Mircalla. "How were you able to set foot into my residence, Lord Greylancer?" Her slender frame convulsed beneath the weight of Zeus's body.

"I suspected your involvement when I was stricken immobile inside the catacombs at Mayerling Castle. Aside from Mayerling's aides, the only one I'd notified of my whereabouts was you. And another: the scent that bound me was similar to your own— the smell you usually conceal with perfume. A certain woman revealed that the incense of great value to me is also made from the same substance—the DNA of the venerable von Hauptmann family. Is that not so, Mircalla *von Hauptmann*?"

The duchess did not answer.

"I was able to enter here undetected by the same trickery that caused the fools to fire their missiles at a mistaken target. Neither your servants nor your surveillance system could observe my coming. They were keeping watch over a different path, while I quietly made my way inside this room." Greylancer flashed a dastardly smile. "I kept a rather incorrigible but skilled craftsman in my employ, you see. Now then, I shall reduce you to dust peacefully if you reveal the name of the traitor who gave you the incense used to produce that anesthetic."

"Very well," said Zeus, his voice strained. "I'll tell you. But a peaceful death be damned. I expect nothing less than a duel."

Brash words, given that he was skewered to the ground by Greylancer's lance, his co-conspirator wedged beneath him. Zeus had thrown down a gauntlet that Greylancer had no cause to take up.

Nevertheless, the great warrior said, "Agreed," and drew out the lance from the chests of the two Nobles. Was this the will or the fate of warriors?

"Do not interfere." Rising to his feet, Zeus raised a hand toward the blood-smeared Mircalla behind him.

A long black whip uncoiled like a serpent and cracked against the ground, sparks flying in every direction. Zeus must have kept it hidden wrapped around his torso.

Another crack, and the whip was joined by another.

When Zeus revealed a third whip, Greylancer thrust his lance.

This was no prod to provoke the enemy, but a full-bodied finishing blow. One whip wound its lash around the lance before the tip could reach its target. Greylancer thrust the lance again. This time the whip unraveled and flew out of the handler's hand. The force of the blow sent Zeus flying backward.

Zeus groaned where he landed. "Twisted the haft, did you?" Although he'd been deprived of one whip, the lashes gripped in his hand now numbered five. "That you can knock me back so easily…you are a formidable warrior. Then how about this?"

Another whip shot out.

What appeared to be a spearhead glanced off Greylancer's lance. His hands stung—the whip was barbed with steel.

"What it lacks in power, it makes up for in dexterity!" The whip circled over Zeus's head and attacked Greylancer again. The Greater Noble repelled the spearhead again, but the supple spear wrapped its tail around the lance like a serpent and tried still to plunge into his heart.

The whip—no, the snake—will not stop no matter how many times I turn it back. How do I kill it?

"Attack!" Zeus shouted and unleashed the five snake whips at the Greater Noble.

A flash of steel streaked through the air in a straight line.

The whips raveled around the lance and threatened to slither up the haft.

Zeus gawked in disbelief.

The whips had stopped.

"You will not have them back," said Greylancer. "Unless my lance tires of them."

With the whips fastened tightly around the haft, Greylancer raised the lance over his head and swung it around. Just once. The five whips twisted around, went slack, and were flung off in the blink of an eye.

"Damn you!" Zeus jumped back as Greylancer thrust his lance once again toward the traitorous Noble's chest.

Suddenly, a pale white figure caught the blade in her bare hands.

"What skill is this?" muttered Greylancer, furrowing his brow.

The duchess, who'd intercepted the deadly attack, let slip a sorrowful smile.

"Do not interfere, Mircalla!" barked Zeus. This was a battle between Noble men.

"Forgive me, Zeus." The woman's voice was barely audible and strained with tension. Her entire body trembled, as she mustered every ounce of strength and tried to stop the blade inching ever closer to her heart. "Quickly!"

Does she mean for me to flee? Zeus bellowed, red-faced, "This is my fight! Stand back, woman!"

"No, my beloved!"

Greylancer gave away a look of amusement upon hearing a hint of affection in the words of the cold-blooded woman. She was prepared to die for the man she loved.

"Your chest wound still bleeds. It will not heal without attention. Quickly, you must escape. I will hold Lord Greylancer here."

Greylancer recognized the meaning behind her words.

If the lance pierced her chest, blood would be spilled. The scent of her blood would likely render Greylancer paralyzed.

"You dare allow a woman to secure your escape?"

Zeus's face flushed. He put a hand on Mircalla's shoulder and seethed, "Back, I say!"

"I will not!"

Greylancer had expected Zeus to push Mircalla aside, but then what?

What transpired next confounded his expectations.

Letting go of the lance, Mircalla lunged forward.

Greylancer retracted his lance, but not before the blade pierced the woman's heart.

So unexpected was this outcome that Greylancer stood transfixed. The blood gushed from Mircalla's wound. Dark pearls of blood sprayed the left side of his face.

Greylancer pressed a hand against his cheek. Black smoke swirled up from between his fingers, as the infernal pain shook his entire being.

"Those burns shall never disappear from your face…" gasped Mircalla. "But Lord Greylancer…the same blood that has scarred you…my blood shall endow you with new powers…Spare him, Greylancer…my spirit…shall remain…eternally grateful."

Mircalla crumpled to the floor, her skeletal remains and white dress besmeared with dust and blood.

Even as Greylancer continued to twitch in pain, he pointed the lance at Zeus's chest, only a jab away from certain death.

"Do it," groaned Zeus. "My surviving by the hand of a woman is a disgrace on the Macula name. Strike me down, Greylancer."

The giant remained still, perhaps stirred by the death of the Noble woman. Beneath the moonlight, a breeze blew around him. Strands of smoke rose up from between his fingers and drifted away into the distance.

Zeus seized the lance tip with both hands and drew himself to his feet. Aiming the blade at his chest, he lunged forward, plunging the lance into his heart just as Mircalla had.

The blood-smeared tip pierced clear through his back.

Greylancer muttered, "Like husband, like wife." As the gentle breeze caressed the moonlight, the warrior suddenly found himself alone in the meadow.

†

Several hours later, a matronly servant left the farmhouse at the edge of the Western Frontier and made her way down the steep hill toward the general store.

At the bottom of the hill, she came upon an uninhabited farmhouse. The moon shone down upon the property, which still hinted at a life abandoned only recently.

The maidservant spotted a caped shadow standing at the gates and nearly fell on her backside. Despite being called slow and dimwitted, she sensed a sinister aura that made her hair stand on end.

Without bothering to turn to address the petrified woman, the shadowy figure asked, "Where is the family that lived here?"

Perhaps some part of the maidservant's heart warned her of the fate that might befall her if she did not answer. Instinctively, her mouth opened. "They moved away three days or so ago," she answered, surprised by how easily the words came out of her mouth.

"I see. There was a blind girl and her brother, a skilled archer. What has become of them?"

"Why, they left together. I don't reckon I know where. The rumor is they headed for the Northern Frontier."

"North," said the shadow in a low murmur.

The woman felt an imperceptible pang in her heart, though she knew not the reason why.

"You have my thanks." The shadow threw down several coins at her feet. It was enough gold for the woman to live on for the rest of her days. "Tell no one of our encounter. If you do…"

The woman shook her head vigorously, knowing well that this unilateral promise was one both intended to keep.

The shadow strode off and disappeared around the corner of the abandoned house. The rattle of a wagon echoed and soon faded into the night.

†

When the woman returned home, the other maidservants of the house took one look at her blanched face and asked what had happened.

"Why you're as pale as death!"

"Darn if you don't look half Noble."

"I'm all right," said the woman to the others gathered around her and hid beneath the tattered bed covers.

Her body glistened with sweat, and she shivered as if stricken by malarial fever.

Yet in her heart, she felt terribly at peace.

At least tonight, she felt strangely comforted that she had encountered someone lonelier than she.

∃

Two days passed. A band of Nobles boarded an OSB aircraft that descended upon the grasslands north of the Capital, whereupon Greylancer and his vassals stormed into the clandestine meeting, killing over twenty OSB—all save one—and capturing the traitorous Nobles.

Greylancer hastened directly for the Privy Council with his captives in tow and demanded the immediate assembly of a council board of inquiry.

The assembled members of the Privy Council examined Greylancer's complaint and were aghast.

The suit disclosed details of the cabal and demanded the dismissal or execution of the current Privy Council members. Also included as part of the demands was the suspension of the planned plasma attack on the Frontier.

Ten members of the Sub-Council gathered in the council chamber to conduct the inquiry. On this night, those Nobles usually in the position of adjudicating such cases found themselves playing the role of defendants.

With Greylancer, who wore a black and white mask over the left side of his face, before them, the accused leveled a barrage of questions against the lone plaintiff.

"What proof do you have? Are you in your right mind? Are you not a suspect yourself for the murder of Chancellor Cornelius?"

To which Greylancer countered:

"I come with evidence and witnesses. I am quite sane. The root of the suspicion against me will become clear in the course of this inquiry."

Then Greylancer's vassals escorted the OSB captive, still in human form, and two members of the Privy Council, who'd vanished days before, to the witness stand. At once, all color drained out of the accused members' faces.

After a medical adviser confirmed that the witnesses were not under the influence of drugs, spells, or other method of supernatural compulsion, each of the witnesses had a turn in confirming the conspiracy.

The testimony of the captured OSB, having no reason to lie, proved more effective in corroborating Greylancer's allegations than those of the two council members.

"In view of these facts, it is evident the current members of the Privy Council have conspired to perpetrate the most heinous of betrayals—to relinquish control of the planet to the OSB." After concluding in a low but forceful voice that shook not only the chambers but also the Privy Council Ministry, Greylancer called for the immediate sentencing of the traitors.

It was plain to anyone that the plaintiff's request was justified. Yet when one of the Sub-Council members asked, "Are there any objections?" one of the defendants—Vice-Chancellor Pitaka—offered a surprising rebuttal.

"Lord Greylancer's accusations in this matter are either all a sham or nothing more than a misunderstanding. No doubt my two colleagues here, much less the OSB, have testified under coercion because they fear for their lives. We are capable of providing ample evidence and testimony to refute the claims made here, but we require several days. But I should think it a waste of time and energy to have to defend ourselves against such preposterous allegations. Nevertheless, these charges, however flimsy, are matters of grave importance that affect the very survival and honor of the Privy Council. I propose, therefore, that our fates be decided by the Ultimate Mind, who has guided us these four thousand years."

Murmurs of surprise erupted from the Sub-Council and judge advocates. Several nodded their approval.

The presiding members retreated to the inner chambers and returned from their deliberations within a minute. "We would like to approve Vice-Chancellor Pitaka's proposal. Lord Greylancer, what say you?"

"I shall defer to your judgment."

Within ten minutes, the Ultimate Mind emerged from an undisclosed location in the bowels of the central government building and entered the chambers unaided.

Though this surrogate of the Sacred Ancestor was a machine comprised of enormous red triangles stood on their points, it exuded a peculiar vitality like that of flesh and blood. "I will hear your statements," it declared.

After the plaintiff and defendants repeated their claims and statements exactly as before, the Ultimate Mind fell silent.

Then, before a minute passed, it answered, "The plaintiff's request is denied. I declare the defendants not guilty."

†

No one dared voice shock or objection. The word of the Sacred Ancestor, even in his surrogate form, was absolute—it was a cardinal rule ingrained in every Noble's bones.

Certainly not every Noble was capable of immortalizing his name in history. What Greylancer did next, however, would cement his already well-chronicled reputation in the annals of history.

"May I inquire the reason?" he asked calmly.

"That is hardly necessary!" shouted Vice-Chancellor Pitaka.

"That will not be necessary," said the Ultimate Mind.

"But—"

"Enough, Lord Greylancer," said the Sub-Council leader, stern. "The Sacred Ancestor's decision is final."

The Greater Noble rose to his feet. "I should like to request another ruling. This is a matter that concerns not only the Nobility but also humanity and the fate of this world."

"A second ruling will change nothing, Lord Greylancer," the Ultimate Mind answered fairly and evenly.

"I ask the Ultimate Mind to deliberate on another matter," said Vice-Chancellor Pitaka, his tone triumphant. "We would like the Privy Council to assume control of the Frontier."

"I see no objection to making it so."

"Vice-Chancellor Pitaka." Greylancer seethed with palpable anger. "I see you have tampered with the Ultimate Mind."

A single wooden spike pierced Greylancer's neck. It had come from the direction of the Ultimate Mind. "You insult me with your accusation, Lord Greylancer," said the machine with the imposing shadow. "This council is now concluded. You are dismissed."

Greylancer pulled the spike from his neck and bit his lip. It was at this moment the warrior vowed to eliminate the members of the Privy Council.

And then the voice added, "This council is declared null and void."

†

It was a deep voice that resonated across the council chambers. Whence had the voice come? Not one Noble directed his attention toward the Ultimate Mind.

The Nobles all looked off in different directions. Heaven and earth.

Their bodies trembled, a phenomenon brought about by the mysterious voice.

It can't be...

Would they utter the name that they had only several occasions to utter in a lifetime?

It can't be...

"Someone has indeed tampered with the Ultimate Mind. Vice-Chancellor Pitaka, perhaps you discovered the operations manual I left behind."

Such a sublime voice. This was no doubt the voice of a missionary from the depths of space.

"It is as you say," acknowledged Pitaka, making no attempt to protest.

There was no outcry toward this admission. The Nobles present felt nothing yet sensed the presence of something extraordinary.

The voice continued, seeming to rain down over them from above. "Vice-Chancellor Pitaka, you have acted treacherously against my will to serve your self-interest. Thus the earlier ruling is null and void. The Frontier will remain under the discretionary powers of the overseers, as it always has. With regard to the war against the OSB, so long as the aliens contend that their invasion is the will of their god and believe that it is just, we must not yield an inch. This is my bidding unto you." The Nobles present bowed their heads in silence. "The rest I leave in your hands. The treachery revealed here today is regrettable. However, the reality before us remains. There is but one path for us to walk."

"Sacred Ancestor." It was Greylancer who spoke up. "Whence have you come? And whence will you go?"

There was no answer.

The Nobles recognized that their venerated ancestor was gone. They stared vacantly as if the presence had retreated again to an unknown place, drawn back to the void inside their hearts. Hidden behind their blank faces was a childlike excitement at having laid eyes on the great man.

†

The traitorous members of the Privy Council were executed on the same day. Greylancer left his adjutants to deal with the aftermath and returned to his childhood home.

Laria greeted him at the door.

Greylancer entered the parlor.

Before he was upon his cherished sofa, his limbs froze. Suddenly, he felt enervated, an intense lethargy invading his bones. "Laria…"

Bathed in the moonlight before him, a gas mask covering his nose and mouth, was Brueghel, Laria's husband.

"Poor Noble, who knew that his stringbean of a brother would be the one to take his life?"

"You stole…this blasted trickery…from Varossa…" said

Greylancer through gritted teeth. The smoke screen and time-deceiving incense could both be traced back to Varossa.

"That's right," replied Brueghel. "In small portions, over time. I hired others to do my bidding, but perhaps Varossa grew wiser to my deceit."

"He…protected you…to the last."

"He is a loyal retainer, such as he is. I expect he will continue to serve Laria and me, grief-stricken as we will be by your death."

"Your backers…have all perished…the Investigation Bureau will soon come for you…"

"At which time, I shall ask Varossa to clone me, to act as a decoy. They will assume that they succeeded in destroying me."

"You intend still…to join with the OSB?"

"Of course. When the OSB conquer this planet, they will hand over full managerial control to me. We have made a pact."

Brueghel's hips wobbled as he unsheathed his blade. Such was the skill of a government toad unpracticed in the ways of swordsmanship.

He inched timidly forward, stopped short of Greylancer's reach, and raised the sword over his head.

In that instant, Greylancer whispered something into the badge on his collar, but Brueghel, too intoxicated by the taste of certain victory, paid no notice.

"Dear Brother, you have always looked down upon my station as civil officer. Perhaps it was you that drove me to conspire with the OSB."

Brueghel swung the long sword.

The blade traced a path that missed wide of its mark. The sword flew out of his hands and skittered across the glass floor as Brueghel fell over on his back.

An unexpected savior had come to Greylancer's aid. It was the swordsman Shizam.

"I came because Gallagher is vulnerable to the time-deceiving incense," said the swordsman, helping the warrior to his feet.

"You…?" said Greylancer, unable to hide his surprise.

"I have been traveling with Gallagher, ever since Lord Mayerling bade me to serve as your retainer."

"Then why did you not say so in the catacombs of Mayerling Castle?"

"I could not bring myself to serve a master who would think nothing of leaving behind a retainer suffering in agony."

"Oh? Then why now?"

"I must carry out my master's orders. As well Gallagher impressed upon me repeatedly that I must not form an opinion by your outward conduct alone."

"Well said," said Greylancer and looked down upon his brother-in-law lying at his feet. After hitting his head in the fall, the floor around Brueghel was smeared with brain matter. A peculiar emotion, one distinct from scorn, came across the warrior's face. Forlornness.

"Brother…finish me…here…" rasped Brueghel as if he were wringing out his last breath. But brain trauma of this sort would not kill a Noble.

"No," roared Greylancer. "You will be punished under Noble law."

"Not that…the fate that awaits me is torture at the hands of half-humans. They harbor a deep-rooted hatred for the Nobility and will inflict that hatred upon my body. Brother…I beg for your mercy. Please, kill me now."

Disregarding his brother-in-law's entreaties and ignoring his bloody outstretched hand, Greylancer said into his comm, "Take this unpardonable traitor into custody."

"My sympathies, Lord Greylancer," said Shizam with a bow.

Before the swordsman could raise his head, an enormous hand shoved him aside. Reeling, Shizam quickly regained his footing and looked up. Greylancer had already vanished in a burst of blinding light.

Brueghel was also gone.

Shizam sent a ferocious glare upward. "A dimensional barrier?" That was the name of the weapon that could confine even immortal Nobles to another dimension for an eternity.

A pale-blue aircraft appeared overhead. Shizam reached for the sword behind his back. He unsheathed the blade and threw it at the enemy in one swift motion. The swordsman watched the sword disappear into the void, but not before cutting a red slash across the aircraft.

In the blink of an eye, the aircraft glowed white-hot, warped into an elongated, twisted shape, and then disappeared like a vision.

Shizam heaved a sigh of relief.

"Who brought me back?" asked Greylancer, suddenly standing next to the swordsman again.

"Lord Greylancer, how did you...?"

"I am armed with all manner of contingencies, thanks to a skilled weaponsmith." Greylancer glanced down at the ground where Brueghel had lain. "Did the OSB come to save Brueghel or destroy him? Their arrival was a blessing in disguise for Brueghel, whichever the case." Looking up at the air, Greylancer asked, "Who was it that brought me back? Have you any idea?"

"I'm afraid I do not," answered Shizam, politely and respectfully. Above him, the vestiges of the brilliant light from whence the OSB came twinkled, then disappeared into the darkness. Then Shizam dropped to one knee and said, "You have saved my life. I shall repay this debt with my life. It would be my honor to serve as your retainer."

"Do as you wish," Greylancer grunted. The effects of the time-deceiving incense were beginning to wear off. "Even a plot to seize the whole world can come to naught in one night—such a pity." Betraying these words, two fangs gleamed from beneath a cynical smile. "We fly for the Frontier tonight. To my territory. To home."

"Yes, my lord."

"After me, Shizam. Do not tarry."

Greylancer strode off toward the Frontier, toward the battleground against the OSB.

The Noble's path was unerring and true.

AFTERWORD

Writing this novel has been a long-cherished dream.

Ever since the *Vampire Hunter D* series began, I have yearned to depict D's world from the perspective of the Noble vampire.

It was only natural, given how the world was created not by humanity, or by D, but by vampires.

In this world, humans are less than slaves—nothing more than livestock in the eyes of the Nobility. Noble vampires, on the other hand, are superior beings. In which case, the protagonist had to be a cold-blooded and arrogant SOB who doesn't feel an ounce of sympathy for the lowly humans. "Ordinary" humans and "ordinary" vampires are not the stuff of heroes in my book.

This explains why, as I penned this story, Greylancer grew more arrogant toward his Noble compatriots. In fact, he draws a clear line between himself and his brethren, holding only the Sacred Ancestor in veneration. As for the rest of the Nobility, he regards them as nothing more than scum, regardless of rank, profession, intellect, or character.

As much as Greylancer, a military man, is forced to keep his destructive self-righteousness in check, he still manages to inspire fear in those around him. He might explode at any moment. Perhaps the only reason keeping Greylancer at his position as Frontier overseer is that he is always in the thick of the action.

The world is teeming with anti-Nobility groups, Noble haters, beasts and monsters roaming the Frontier, thieves and bandits.

No friends or allies. To Greylancer, humans and Nobles alike are all enemies to be slaughtered.

Does that not make him a crazed murderer? Close, but not exactly. In fact, his compatriots hold him in awe, according him the appellation *Noble* Greylancer because he stoically refuses to allow others to rival him. This is manifested in his sense of duty as overseer to his subjects.

He is bound to protect the human weaklings.

It is Greylancer's responsibility to defend humanity—beings that a vampire might typically trample on, tear to shreds, and feed upon—from the clutches of monsters, villainous humans, and wayward Nobles. In other words, Greylancer must protect humanity from himself.

Tragedy or comedy?

It doesn't matter which. Either suits Greylancer just fine.

As Greylancer kills, feeds upon humans, turns savior, feels anger, laughs and cries, I believe readers experience his journey along with him. That is the kind of character the Noble Greylancer is.

—Hideyuki Kikuchi
December 2010,
while watching *Dracula* (1958)

BONUS:
AN IRREPLACEABLE
EXISTENCE

1

Lord Voyevoda's request necessitated a trip to the scrap metal yard. Many of the orders I'd received of late had been troublesome, especially those coming from his lordship. Apparently he was on the battlefield, driving tanks in the armored cavalry.

There were scrap metal yards north and west of the city of Cité, but the one up north tended to yield better finds. The upper class was concentrated in the ghettoes north and south. Although I lived east, the pass issued to me by City Hall afforded me free passage.

I ambled beneath the steel framework towering diagonally over the entrance of the yard and felt my eyes sting.

I squeezed my eyes shut. When I managed to look up, countless plumes were rising up from the cityscape shaped like an inverted minimido into the gray-blue sky. The jagged protrusions comprising the skyline were the famed chimneystacks of Cité. The sky would lose its blue luster in no time.

Why was this scrap metal yard stretching three kilometers square even called a yard at all? It had been a subject of debate since the first metal fragments were cast away here. I believe this place would more accurately be called a dump.

Probably because the first scrap metals discarded here were still strewn about, though they were displayed with some meaning and sentiment.

Others must have followed suit, as the stairs, which took me down a hundred meters to the bottom, were fashioned from steel beams stacked one on top of the next.

I turned right at the junk pile of coils, rusted generators, cracked condensers, and walked a ways past the mounds of obsolete computer motherboards towering on either side of me like mountain ranges, until I spied an inky silhouette in the shadows on the right.

The figure was veiled in haze, so I could not make out its arms or legs. Doubtful that it was a fellow scavenger on the hunt for precious metals, I stopped and waited for him to make the first move. Man or woman? Probably neither. Certainly non-humans were capable of thieving and killing.

As I debated whether to walk past or call out, a blue hand emerged from somewhere about the dark figure's chest. Its gaudy blue hue served to heighten the theatrical and surreal air. But my curiosity lay in whatever the wiry index finger pointed at.

It was pointing toward the corridor on the left, much like the one from which this dark figure had emerged.

Trying not to appear terribly interested, I ambled before the corridor and stole a quick look. Though I'd intended only a glance, my eyes fastened upon the figure lying in the middle of the corridor about fifteen meters away.

I froze, not because the female figure was naked, but because her prostrate body disrupted the orderliness of the place. Her haphazard presence relegated the yard to a dump.

My attention instantly shifted to her body. Her gleaming black skin, the rivets hammered into her shoulders, elbows, and neck captivated my artistic sensibilities honed over forty-something years. The left arm was exquisite, but the right arm and neck dangled from the body, each barely held together by one rivet. There were crescent-shaped holes around the right elbow, knee, and ankle where the rivets had gone missing.

"Who created her?" I heard myself ask. My voice sounded distant.

The woman was perfect. Her finely burnished hair, graceful

neck, a shiny black back that would reflect lightning, the curves from her hips down to the ankles were like a dream. What impressed me most was the beauty with which the rivets and screws had been driven. This particular craftsmanship was rivaled only by the 3,004th descendant of the Zaitan line, and myself.

Ah, just look at the workmanship of her face!

I glanced back to ask why the black figure had alerted me to this woman's presence, but the figure had vanished.

When I drew closer and looked down upon the woman, I felt something wasn't quite right.

She was not perfect. But it was not because of some flaw or damage.

Maybe something is wrong with her other side. I put a hand on her shoulder to sit her up, when I sensed the presence of others behind me.

They quickly surrounded me.

"What do you think you're doing?" The voice of the young woman clanged like an alarm bell.

"Nothing," I answered, not even bothering to turn around. I knew what they were doing here. It wasn't at all strange that a woman was among junkyard bandits. After all, we lived in an age where women won mixed-gender weightlifting competitions. Using the Tendo breathing method, women were capable of transporting a hundred, even two hundred kilos of scrap metal in their slender arms. Three women working in concert were capable of carrying over a ton.

"Nice find," said the voice kindly. A faint scent of perfume wafted into the air. "But we had an eye on her first. You will have to leave her here."

"Your voice sounds very hoarse." Pulling the robotic woman's arm over my shoulder, I drew her to her feet. Solving her mysteries would have to wait till I evacuated her to a more appropriate location. "It can't be the effects of the smoke alone. You'd best have a doctor take a look at your throat."

One of the bandits behind me kicked my female companion in the hip, which shook my shoulders.

"Please leave her here," the female bandit requested again. She would likely apologize and ask for my forgiveness in that same gentle tone when she shredded me to pieces.

This was going nowhere. At this rate, we would only continue to inhale the filthy air from the city. "Here are my terms. Come to 1313 Yami Street in the Shin Shin District in two weeks, at which time I will give you—"

Before I could offer another woman in place of this one, the bandits cried out in unison, "Yami Street! Shin Shin District? Then you must be—"

"Master Craftsman Monde," I answered. And before the second chorus of cries had died down, I slipped past my captors and turned around.

The bandits were all women wearing long dresses and gloves, no doubt daughters of good families living in the core wards. Their masks also appeared to be expensive—too expensive, in fact, for merely concealing their identities from witnesses to their bad deeds.

Before turning the corner with my prize, I said, "In two weeks then." The bandits did not answer. The sky had turned violet from soot and smoke.

†

Upon returning to the workshop, I found Shwann inside. He was my part-time assistant. By "part-time," I mean that he was not officially in my employ, so he came and went as he pleased. Still I did not refuse his help when he offered it. Shwann was as adept at fastening rivets and screws as I. All he needed was to improve his welding technique, and he might have passed for a twenty-year veteran of the trade.

As I suspended the woman from chains, I asked Shwann what he made of this creation.

"She seems odd," he answered, exactly as I had expected. It was not that his answer was obvious. In fact, if you were to ask the craftsmen in the city, only one in a hundred would answer likewise—in other words, zero of them would, given how there were exactly fifty craftsmen approved by the city.

Listening to the beautiful squeak of the ceiling pulleys, I went about the work of securing the woman's body in chains, a task that required the sensitivity of a poet, when a whistle issued forth from one of the speaking tubes hanging from the wall. It was a gentleman who'd called previously about an odd job too small to consider taking on. After inquiring his name as a matter of courtesy, I explained that I was busy and slammed the lid over the cone. I received no less than a thousand such minor requests each year.

I cast a long, unabashed look at the woman. The only time I'd felt any desire for a woman's naked body was the month immediately after I'd fired up the coals in this workshop for the first time. Shwann still could not look at such a sight without blushing. It was this innocence that had compelled me to take him under my wing.

"Oh? Odd how?" I asked, the devil getting into me. His delicate face flushed again with embarrassment, imbuing him with a look of insolence.

Yet he did not fail me with his answer.

"The left side of the throat."

I nodded my approval. There was indeed a tiny hole just above her carotid artery. In fact, there were two. Discovering them amid the jet-black gleam of the woman's steel skin was no easy feat.

"What beautiful punctures," he said, fascinated, as I tried to imagine what kind of punch and hammer was used to produce them.

No doubt the tools had been extraordinarily dense, sharp, and heavy. Were they tools from the so-called "stars in the sky" people were talking about? Shwann's question brought me back from my reverie.

"What do you intend to do with her? Will you fill in the holes and restore her to her original pristine form?"

I shook my head, though that task might also have been to Shwann's benefit. "No, not that."

"Then why did you bring her here? Do you plan to use some of her parts to build Lord Voyevoda's requested item?"

"The wound on this woman's neck—wouldn't you like to recreate the thing that carried out this exquisite workmanship?"

"Wasn't it done with a punch and hammer?" he asked.

"To the eye, yes. But my instincts tell me otherwise. We must suspend our work for Lord Voyevoda. I will let his servant know immediately."

"He will not be pleased. Forgive me, but Lord Voyevoda has been the greatest champion of your work."

"In twenty years, the greatest champion I've never met." I felt my lips curl into a self-mocking smile. No matter how much work he commissioned or the size reward he promised in return for my creations, I could not bring myself to warm to a supporter whose face I'd never seen and who always conducted his business via servants. Even his address was unknown to me. "I will deliver his order by the promised date. But we must work around the clock. You may leave if you're not interested."

"Not a chance." Shwann rolled the sleeves of his white cotton shirt up to his elbows. The distorted reflection of his hands— hands too pale to know physical labor—danced like mystical creatures over the woman's shiny black stomach. I was struck by the strangeness of the scene but knew not to whom, Shwann or the iron woman herself, this feeling should be attributed.

†

Our first order of business was to examine the wound on the woman's throat.

Extrapolating the shape of the tool that produced these holes based on the depth and diameter, as well as their internal measurements, required a full day.

While it was all strictly conjecture, I stuck the drawing I'd sketched based on the collected data in front of Shwann's nose. "What do you think?"

"I don't know…"

"That makes two of us," I said.

"But who would—why would someone do such a thing?"

"You don't know?"

"No."

"Neither do I. It boggles the mind. But frankly, I'm not surprised. The kinds of jobs that enliven a craftsman are all like this."

"Just what is it that the dark figure from the scrap yard wants you to accomplish?"

"Who knows? Perhaps I am already carrying out his plan without even knowing. In any case, if we begin to stray, we will need some redirection. Let's pray that he will appear again when that time comes. What are you looking at?"

I peered down at Shwann's hands. He was staring at my recreation of the wound.

"Master Monde, your rendering is brilliant as well. But this time…" He cast an admiring look at the woman's neck. "Her wound is more beautiful."

"Let's get back to work."

"On Lord Voyevoda's item?"

"Fool."

"But—" Shwann blurted out. "We know what put this mark on the woman's throat. What more is there to do?"

"Are you satisfied? The thing that created this wound, which so enthralls you, is not what we guessed."

"Well, no, but…" Shwann fell silent.

I fixed a hard look on his pale face. Whoever this young man was, it was unlikely he'd ever had to confront such a gaze. "Consider this your opportunity to prove yourself a full-fledged craftsman," I said, envisioning that blue flame burning in every artist's heart. My wife, when she was alive, used to chide me that it symbolized perversity.

"With pleasure, Master Monde. I swear by the gleam of Liber steel."

"You will recreate the item that made this wound. I shall conceive the being that wields it. Only when we accomplish this will my ambition, and the wishes of my strange patron, become reality. Should your measurements be off by even a millimeter, the pressure applied on the chisel too strong or not strong enough, or the temperature of the coals even a degree off, the whole of my work will come to nothing. Whether we succeed in earning what will likely be a peculiar reward from a most peculiar patron or become the laughingstock of his world—rests entirely on your skill."

Shwann's knees appeared to buckle as the gravity of my words registered in his mind. I half expected him to fold under the pressure and run.

But my mysterious young assistant—whose past was unknown to me—put a hand on his minutely detailed gold buckle, swept back his gold locks with his other hand, and answered exactly as I had expected. "On the gleam of Liber steel and my soul, you have my word."

What Shwann made of this task, I did not know. I only know that he did not take this challenge lightly.

First, he recreated the deadly weapon by pouring molten iron into the woman's wound. Gauging the eutectic temperature and just the right moment to remove the objects from the mold requires no small amount of skill and concentration even for me, but Shwann managed it deftly.

The moment the items were submerged in the vat of distilled water, clouds of steam hissed and billowed in the air, forming a faint rainbow in the corner of the workroom. Shwann and I stopped for a moment and stared, mesmerized by the color spectrum arching across the room until it faded like a mirage.

As I looked down at the tiny items on the tray, I heard Shwann ask from behind, "What do you think they are?"

"I haven't a clue," I answered. In all my years as master crafts-man, never had I seen anything that was so outside my realm of knowledge and experience.

Two objects, no more than two centimeters long, with pointed ends. What in the world could they be?

"Find out how these two might best be fitted," I said, offering what I thought to be the next plausible step.

"Might I employ the services of a metal burnisher first?"

"Yes, all right." I nodded, trying to conceal my embarrassment. It had completely slipped my mind! Once cast into shape, the metals had to be carefully polished by the hand of an expert. The god of smithing would never forgive me for such an elementary lapse in logic.

Ever since I had chosen the path of craftsman, my metal bur-nisher had always been Shwalde, a woman from the Yufu district, where the rowhouses stretched ten kilometers like dominoes.

The combustible engine popped and wheezed as the steam car carried us to a street lined with brick tenement houses.

The old woman, who was over three hundred years old, wel-comed us into her cramped apartment home on the top floor of one of the tenements.

"Now, what are these odd things you've brought me?" Shwalde asked suspiciously. Cité's most skilled burnisher took the deadly weapons in her hands and examined them, squinting beneath the colored light streaming in through the stained glass skylight in the ceiling.

"Any idea what they are?" I asked as if we'd met for the first time.

"I seem to recall a very long time ago…" Shwalde shook her head. "No, perhaps not. I've become forgetful in my old age. Still…"

"Still?"

"I can't shake this feeling that they're very dangerous. I'll take extra care in polishing them."

"I shall be most grateful."

After Shwalde promised to finish the job within three days, I stood from my chair to part ways.

But the old woman did not follow. Her head bobbed against her chin first and then the rest of her body fell forward onto the table without a sound.

The poor woman was as light in my arms as if she were made of tinfoil, as Shwann helped me carry her to her bed. Thankfully, she came to before we had to give her water and medicine, which was a great relief to us.

"It's my lungs," Shwalde explained. "But don't you worry, I'll finish the job as promised."

"Can we find you some medicine?"

"Don't you think I've tried already? Never mind that, would you mind bringing *them* over here, lad?"

Shwann grabbed the weapons from the table and placed them in her wrinkled hands.

Saying nothing, I watched her fingers slowly close around them.

"I am at peace," Shwalde said, as if in a dream. By the looks of her, it appeared to be a good dream. "What we have here seems to be very dangerous and precious at the same time. Why do they calm me so? Now how much longer are you going to stare at me in my sorry state? Go on home."

†

Upon receiving word on the morning of the appointed day, Shwann headed out for the old woman's home.

When my assistant returned several hours later, I was studying the liquid metal bubbling from the window of the smelting furnace, pleased with the exceptional quality of the coal and iron he'd procured this year.

"Shwalde has been taken to the hospital," Shwann informed me upon his return. Holding a small package with both hands in my direction, he continued, "She gave this to me at the hospital. She was clutching it in her arms and did not let go until she saw me."

I took the package and asked, "What do you think it is?" despite knowing the answer. I felt a desperate need to achieve some modicum of mutual understanding.

I set the package on the worktable and opened it. The tiny lethal weapons glinted inside. Was the fact that I had not yet reached Shwalde's age the reason why the burnished items did not appear any more sinister?

I refrained from asking Shwann's opinion.

"I believe I know how they are fitted," my assistant said a bit bashfully.

"Oh? And?"

"I made a model out of clay and plaster. May I show it to you?"

"Of course."

As Shwann turned on his heels to retrieve the item, the doorbell jangled violently.

I hurried to the several dozen speaking tubes sticking out of the wall, removed the lid covering the cone and tube connected to the entrance, and asked, "Who's there?"

"We made your acquaintance at the scrap metal yard up north a week ago," answered a clarion voice. An image of the ladies in their long white gloves and elegant dresses floated into my mind. The high-rise district, from which they came, held lavish balls every night.

After waving Shwann off, I said into the speaking tube, "Forgive me, but I have nothing to offer you in exchange for the woman. You'll have to wait another week."

"I'm afraid that won't do."

Several seconds later, the building was rocked by a loud explosion. The heavy thud of the outer door falling inward shook the speaking tube in my hand. The outer door was made of iron. Just how had the young ladies gotten their hands, so delicate that they might break, on such a large quantity of high explosives?

The door separating the workshop from the residence was three times thicker than the outer door. I undid the lock and waited for Shwann.

Boom! The door shook.

The door buckled inward, as cracks formed around the hinges and streaked across the wall. *Boom!*

The door fell with a dull thud.

A woman made of steel stepped over the rusty fallen door and rushed into the workshop first. She was a meticulous female recreation down to every last eyelash and strand of fluttering hair. The workmanship on her jet-black skin, despite paling in comparison to Shwalde's technique, was extraordinary.

"Whose creation is this?" I asked the shadows in flowing dresses standing behind the steel woman.

"A craftsman who works for me," answered an exceedingly beautiful girl. I was blinded by the brilliant glare of the stone hanging from her necklace. It was not an adamantine spar, but a gem. "Now how about returning the other woman to me?"

"I haven't finished examining her yet."

"That's a matter of your convenience. I insist you honor our agreement."

"According to our agreement, I still have another week."

"I'm afraid you will have to accommodate our schedule. The woman is being sold earlier than expected."

"What am I to do?" I cried out, gripped by a sudden worry over the girl's future. "Now look, it's not too late. There's still time for anyone who wants to leave. You must understand you are about to rob a craftsman."

A wave of unrest stirred among the young women.

A diminutive shadow quietly crept back toward the doorway. It was a girl wearing a red jewel at her chest.

"Traitor! Turncoat!" cried a chorus of shrill voices.

"We let you into our group, you ungrateful wench. You lower district girls are rotten beyond saving!"

Tears rolled down the girls' faces.

"Get her!"

The steel woman lunged at the traitorous girl. As the girl tried to escape, the android grabbed her arms with one hand, pulled her close, and wrung her neck.

The red jewel from dead girl's chest clattered on the ground.

"We wept for her," the girls turned to me and said as if in defense of their friend's cruel end. Then with the steel woman leading the way, one by one, they stepped across the fallen door and entered the workshop. When the last of the intruders cleared the door, I raised my hand.

The door was lifted upright and back in its original position.

As the girls cried out in disbelief, I heard Shwann call to me from behind.

"What is it?" I asked without turning around.

"According to my calculations, *this.*"

I felt something heavy being placed in my outstretched hand.

The girls' whispers turned to gasps as I watched their elegant silhouettes dance like a mirage. Suddenly, the look in their eyes wavered from menace to terror and another emotion.

One of the girls cried out, prompting the steel woman to march toward me.

My only worry was that the furnace door would not open on command, but my invention worked like a charm.

I pressed the button on the remote control handed to me by Shwann and watched the molten metal pour down from the smelting furnace and over the steel woman. The red heat spread across her black skin. Her hand, dripping steel like blood, reached out and came within a finger-length of my chest before receding along with the rest of her melting body into the cascade of liquid metal. Within seconds, she disappeared into the orange-colored current flowing toward the door. For many years, the cement floor of the workshop had been severely slanted toward the entrance and was badly in need of repair. So terrified was I by my own prospect of death that I did not notice the shrieks of the girls being burned and swallowed by the lava flow that swept them screaming out of my workshop.

"Such a cruel turn..." Shwann muttered.

Though I might have ignored him, I asked, "Do you think so?" curious about how he might answer.

"No." His unmitigated response was filled with a greater brutality than I possessed. It was in this moment that I intuited this city would in time become home to the greatest craftsman in history.

†

Soon, a rumor floated around the city that investigators had taken up the case of the disappearance of the young women. The rumor was probably true. I didn't give a damn. After being swept up in the molten flow and into the drainage pipes, their skin and bones should have ended up in the "roving lake" that is said to exist somewhere belowground.

From the time the sun rose in the violet smoke-filled sky to sundown, I spent my days staring, with unflagging fascination, at Shwann's creation.

One day I asked, "What do you think they are?"

"I believe they're teeth," was Shwann's answer. The two pointed objects that had so beautifully left their mark on the woman's throat were fitted on either side of a steel model of a dental arch.

"I believe you're right. But have you ever seen such vicious bestial fangs in your life?"

"No." Shwann's green eyes were lit with curiosity. "But there is no mistaking. These are what left the marks on this woman here."

"Exactly. By God, I am stumped. No human that I know has fangs like these. Which is why I am thinking about creating a human that might rightly wield these teeth."

My young assistant was struck speechless, but only for a moment. "That's—that's incredible, Master Monde. I hadn't even considered such an idea. But you will be bringing into existence a being not of this world, an act Lord Voyevoda strictly forbids."

"Again with Lord Voyevoda. In the past, thousands of craftsmen died by the guillotine for resisting the edicts of a certain higher noble—beheaded for refusing to aid House Voyevoda's effort in the Million Year War against an indeterminate enemy. I refuse to cower against such tyranny. On my name and honor,

I will neither cower nor back down. Shwann, if you do not feel likewise, I bid you leave now."

The young man took one step back and bowed his head deeply. The invincible smile that came across his face was the only answer I needed.

From that day began what I recognized as the challenge of a lifetime.

Two teeth must form the basis of an entire being.

From the shape of the lower and upper jaws, facial form to the size of the nasal and ocular cavities—we could not be even one millimeter off.

Holing myself up in the musty library, I pored over tomes written by the sages of antiquity and, using a calculator and protractor that were heretofore of little use me, extrapolated the exact measurements of each of the required parts.

On the eve of our appointed day to begin casting, Shwann and I sat at the table and stared in silence at the teeth.

As the sky turned from violet to blue, the black teeth gleamed in the moonbeams filtering in from the skylight. What the girls must have felt when they'd first discovered them!

Suddenly, Shwann snatched the black teeth off the table and shot a piercing gaze at the fangs. He was not yet a full-fledged craftsman. I caught his hand trying to sink the teeth into his own neck and slapped him across the face. When I slapped him for a seventh time, Shwann came back to himself.

"What...what did I do?" he groaned, to which I shook him by the shoulders and said, "Don't. You must never repeat what you just attempted. Only the creature that wields these teeth is permitted such a violent act."

"Yes, I understand now."

I stroked the boy's hair, pushing my fingers through his gold locks like a hydraulic tank mowing down reeds.

"Perhaps it would have been kinder to send you back to your family," I muttered, looking up at the purple constellations through the skylight in the bedroom. "But no. I don't know where your parents are. I'm not even certain you have parents. In the first place, the very concept of parents is foreign to me. I was a test tube baby, you see. Though I do not know the female and male donors, I harbor no resentment. At least, they had talents worthy of passing on to me." Whether Shwann understood or even heard me at all was a mystery. When I turned back from my soliloquy, the lad had bundled himself in blankets next to me and was sound asleep as if he were not even breathing.

†

The next three months of suffering to complete the face is certainly worth chronicling here.

When it came time to mold the facial skeleton, I began to doubt my own talents. If my measurements and imagination proved accurate, the completed face should look exactly like the drawing before me. But was I skilled enough to carve these same lips, nasal bridge, eyes, and above all these very pupils into steel?

I must have considered abandoning my name, rank, and workshop and running away to the oft-rumored neighboring city over a hundred times.

The chisel in my hand trembled relentlessly as I carved the cheekbones, and the lips that I'd managed to sculpt after much agony let out a scornful laugh audible only to me. The eyeballs reflected the image of a middle-aged man balled up in a fetal position in a corner of the workshop, terrified by the enormous task before him.

But it was this task that also saved me.

Exhausted, Shwann fell asleep with his arms and head spread over the table cluttered with my many failed attempts to produce a face. With more faces scattered about his feet, Shwann looked like a gravedigger who'd enjoyed a night of merrymaking with skulls in a cursed underground cemetery.

He came in the dead of night. I heard the door creak open, but I was too hopeless and exhausted to raise my head.

I sensed the visitor bypass the countless faces scattered about, stop before my desk, and take up my latest creation that I'd set down next to me.

"Exquisite," I heard him say.

I lifted my weary head. Was there a savior that reached out to every man drowning in the depths of despair? Even if that savior was a faceless specter shrouded in a shadowy cloak?

"You have my esteem and trust in your abilities. You must continue the work you have started. Here is my payment for your troubles."

I glimpsed a blue hand—the same blue hand I'd seen at the scrap metal yard—withdraw a satchel from the shadows of his cloak, and I felt myself warming to this black figure at last. The satchel left on the desk contained fifty gimli coins.

After watching the shadow stride out into the dark gray world, I strained to stand.

Somehow I staggered to my feet.

I shambled over to the table where Shwann slept.

"Let's get back to work," I said. My assistant picked himself up without complaint.

Three days later, the face was complete. Then on a snowy day three months later, I hosted an unveiling ceremony for my creation.

Shwann was the only audience in attendance. The black figure had not visited again since that night three months and three days prior.

After Shwann alone applauded the unveiling, he gazed at the finished product and asked, "Does such a creature exist?" His voice had the hollow ring of a man for whom the answer was obvious.

With his hair combed neatly back, his face exuded a refinement rarely seen in upper-class society. The well-to-do citizens of Cité might have seen it differently.

I'll say no more about his visage. The parts I had labored over the most were the ties and wrinkles of the cloak. I doubted the being himself would complain about my craftsmanship.

His forward-bent stance with one foot forward and arms crossed over his chest had also been extrapolated from the fangs.

At first glance, he looked as human as you and I, from his hairstyle to his facial features, his cloak and the garments underneath. Yet no human grew fangs the likes of which this creature wielded now.

"So these are the fangs that punctured the woman's throat," said Shwann, haggard. I nodded. "But for what purpose? There is absolutely nothing to be gained, that I can think of, from doing so."

"Why don't we ask the victim directly?"

Shwann gasped, perhaps not thinking to ask.

"Bring the woman to me," I said, but Shwann shook his head.

"She's not here. She has been missing since yesterday."

I stared at my assistant's drawn face and asked, "Has this happened before?"

"Yes," he answered. "While we were working on the face, she sometimes went into the other room. But she may have slipped out of the house several times this last month. And I say *may* because she has always returned to her room after two or three days, and I have not actually seen her outside."

"Why do you suppose she's run away?"

"I imagine she doesn't want to be wounded again."

I nodded in agreement and asked, "Do you think she will return soon?"

"There's just no telling, although I understand this is rare."

"Do you think you can find her?" I asked, reluctant to order him outright.

Shwann bowed and hurried out of the workshop straightaway.

Within ten minutes, the front door burst open and a gang of police officers stormed into the workshop.

"May I help you, officers?" I asked, affecting civility.

An officer distinguished by his spiral moustache stepped forward and unfolded a metallic-colored document. "By order of the court of Cité, we are here to search the residence of Master

Craftsman Monde on Yami Street, Shin Shin District. We have a report filed by ninety-five-year-old Ver Non of 22,605,984 north high-rise district, claiming that his seventeen-year-old niece Ayla Non and nine friends disappeared three months ago after visiting your home…"

I felt my lips curl almost imperceptibly.

†

I had not reported the deaths of the female bandits. Though an interrogation would no doubt find me justified in my actions, clearing my name would take some time, especially against the word of a well-to-do citizen of the high-rise district. There was also the risk that the police might have been bribed. Even if the truth were revealed in time, that might be after I'd been tortured, with molten lead poured into my bloody back at the hands of the police.

I had only one option. Death. But it would afford me the time I needed before my execution.

I interrupted the bearded man from pronouncing the date of my so-called questioning and confessed to the charges. "I confess to the murder of the women as charged. I understand that the proper punishment for my crime is death. But I wish to exercise the second of three privileges accorded all confessors—two weeks of unconditional probation."

After the bearded man agreed to my terms, I was made to sign several documents and was spared immediate arrest.

All I could do now was wait.

As the day wore into night and still Shwann did not return, I began to wonder if I'd sent him on a fool's errand.

I woke up in the dead of night for some unknown reason. I crept out of my bedroom and into the workshop.

A mysterious presence stood in the corner of the room, where the steel woman lay crumpled at his feet trying to back away from the shadow's clutches.

I called out my assistant's name, but he did not appear.

"So you have returned…of your own volition," I said to the woman. Naturally, she did not answer. "You escaped on your own and chose to return on your own. For what unearthly reason? Just what is it about *this*," I said, gesturing toward the fanged being, "that so terrifies and attracts you? I can only think that you too are some unreal presence who is connected somehow to this—my unreal creation."

I left the couple in the workshop and returned to the main house.

Shwann soon returned from his search, hanging his head. "I could not find her."

I led the lad into the workshop, whereupon he gawked, dumbfounded at the sight of the steel woman cowering before my fanged creation. After I explained that she had returned here on her own, Shwann shot me an admiring gaze and said, "How I aspire to your skill, Master Monde. I hope to become the kind of craftsman capable of bringing the unreal into being someday." He ran a tender hand along the woman's steel skin, until his fingers stopped at the side of the neck, where the mystery had all begun and would take another turn.

I noticed the cause of his consternation before Shwann spoke. "Master Monde, next to the holes…are more puncture wounds."

On the volcanic flames of Yoga, I swear that the punctures were not there when I had found her earlier. "These must be new. Apparently the same forbidden act is being repeated in our absence."

"For how much longer?"

"I do not know."

"For what purpose?"

When I did not answer, Shwann walked calmly toward the worktable and snatched up the hand drill. Before I could intercede, he plunged the drill into his neck. Drawing it out, Shwann tilted his neck so that I might see. "Anything different?"

"No," I answered. I detected only a tiny discoloration on his milky skin but nothing that might reveal any earthly reason for anyone to puncture a woman's neck.

"What now, Master Monde?"

"I imagine our client will be by to collect them."

"These beings belong here," said Shwann, shooting me a defiant look for the first time. "This fanged creature is your masterpiece."

"I have already been paid a fee."

"You must not," said Shwann, his tone growing angry. "I cannot bear to see you hand over your creation—no, the product of our first collaboration, however small my part, to some stranger."

"Only when we deliver our products to the client do we earn the right to call ourselves craftsmen. Apparently your time under my apprenticeship has been wasted." Then, trying to suppress any hint of sentimentality, I bade him never to darken my door again. Shwann opened his mouth as if to speak. Had he appealed to our relationship, I might have gone to my grave despising him. But the young man had more dignity than that. Saying nothing, Shwann took one step back, bowed deeply, and showed himself out of my workshop.

†

It was two days later that my client arrived at last.

The metallic couple stood before the black-shrouded visitor, as ghostly blue flames from the gas lamps danced off their steel skin.

"I am greatly satisfied. A recompense for your labor." The black figure dropped a heavy satchel on the table.

I slid the satchel back and said, "I'm afraid I have no use for money."

"So I have heard. I regret the trouble I have caused."

"Then perhaps you'll answer one question."

"Please." The visitor bowed, which aroused a strange feeling in me. I know now that it was a paradoxical feeling. Something told me that this man was incapable of displaying such deference.

How could this be? It was the familiar gesture of a man I knew well.

"Your previous visit also took place when my apprentice was gone." The black figure might have pulled away had I attempted any large movement. Instead I stepped on the pedal that I'd rigged before my client's arrival, and a hook swung down from the ceiling and tore off the hood shrouding his face. I had calculated the trajectory of the hook according to the man's presumed height.

Recognizing the face, I grunted, "What is the meaning of this?"

"Who is it that you see?"

"Shwann." What was he doing shrouded in a black overcoat?

"Yes, that's right." The young man smiled.

And then innumerable footsteps surged like a tide from the entrance, and a mob crashed through the door. There were more of them this time. The policemen that packed into the room exceeded a hundred.

Shrouded in black, Shwann remained collected as one might expect, and I too remained perfectly still, this time stunned by another face that confronted me. I uttered a name I did not expect to repeat. "Shwann?"

"That is the name of your apprentice." Shwann brushed back his blue cloak, revealing gold insignia on the shoulder and chest of his armor underneath. Engraved on his chest was the insigne of a noble family that might be forever emblazoned in anyone's memory.

It was the insigne of House Voyevoda.

"My name is Schranz, the 249,974,031st Lord of House Voyevoda," said Shwann solemnly. "I became your apprentice because I thought it a shame to lose your skill and these creations with no one to succeed you. Your creations may serve my House in battle, but I will not allow them to pass into the hands of anyone who refuses to show his face."

When I turned to where Shwann pointed, the second black-shrouded Shwann had pulled his hood over his face. "Forgive me, but I cannot reveal my identity at this time."

Stepping forward, Shwann—or Lord Voyevoda—grabbed hold of the man's hood and cried in disbelief the moment he pulled it off. The shouts of the policemen and my own that followed shook the workshop.

The black-shrouded figure now revealed a face that was mine. "Who do you see now?" he asked.

"Master Monde," Shwann gasped.

"Indeed, I am he."

The eyes of everyone in the room ricocheted between me and my doppelganger in the black shroud, as Shwann said, "But which is—"

"Do not be alarmed," said my double as he pulled the hood over his face again. "Who am I now?" He pulled back the hood, and it was Shwann again. "And now?"

As he pulled the hood on and off again, he assumed the face of the policeman next to Shwann. And then the policemen next to him, and next to him.

Before any of us recovered our senses, the man, his face shrouded in the hood again, said, "I am each and every one of you. As well as the selves you do not know, and the totality of the worlds you have yet to know. One such world desires your two creations as its own. There, they together shall become an irreplaceable existence in the world's history."

"Where is this world you speak of?" asked Shwann in a thread-thin voice.

"I do not know, for my part is but to collect them and send them on their journey." A blue hand rose and beckoned.

The policemen cleared a path, and my two creations rose several centimeters from the floor and glided to their places on either side of the black-shrouded figure.

Suddenly, Shwann swung his right hand over his head and brought down the gold knife and plunged it into the black figure's chest.

"Now if you will excuse us." The black figure bowed. The

knife in his chest quivered. As the figure turned and headed for the door, the two steel shadows followed. No one dared pursue or stand in their way. We had all been paralyzed by terror.

As I watched the steel woman drift past me, I felt as if a spike had been driven into my eye.

My shock did not dissipate for a long while after they left and the echo of their footsteps faded. "Did you see?" I asked Lord Schranz Voyevoda—no, Shwann—my entire body dripping in a cold sweat. "What will befall the world after their arrival? I fear its history will be a cursed one."

"What did you see?" Shwann asked.

Try as I might to answer with the dignity of a master addressing his apprentice, my voice quivered. I said, "The woman also grew fangs."

†

In the end, my fate traced a path up the platform steps to the guillotine. The young lord did not appear at my beheading. When the cold blade was brought down upon my neck, I felt gratified for my fortunate end.

I intuited that those who would encounter my creations would never be so fortunate as to greet a death as peaceful and swift as mine.

ABOUT THE AUTHOR

Hideyuki Kikuchi was born in Chiba in 1949. He graduated from the Aoyama Gakuin University of Law and, inspired by H. P. Lovecraft, began publishing supernatural fiction in the early 1980s. One of the most prolific authors in the field, Kikuchi has published over three hundred books and still produces multiple novels per year. He has enjoyed international success as a novelist, and much of his work has been adapted for manga and anime. Kikuchi is the author of the ongoing series *Vampire Hunter D*. *Wicked City*, *A Wind Named Amnesia*, and *Dark Wars: The Tale of Meiji Dracula* number among his works available in English.

HAIKASORU
THE FUTURE IS JAPANESE

VIRUS: THE DAY OF RESURRECTION
—SAKYO KOMATSU

In this classic of Japanese SF, American astronauts on a space mission discover a strange virus and bring it to Earth, where rogue scientists transform it into a fatal version of the flu. After the virulent virus is released, nearly all human life on Earth is wiped out save for fewer than one thousand men and a handful of women living in research stations in Antarctica. Then one of the researchers realizes that a major earthquake in the now-depopulated United States may lead to nuclear Armageddon...

SELF-REFERENCE ENGINE
—TOH ENJOE

This is not a novel.
This is not a short story collection.
This is Self-Reference ENGINE.

Instructions for Use: Read chapters in order. Contemplate the dreams of twenty-two dead Freuds. Note your position in space-time at all times (and spaces). Keep an eye out for a talking bobby sock named Bobby Socks. Beware the star-man Alpha Centauri. Remember that the chapter entitled "Japanese" is translated from the Japanese, but should be read in Japanese. Warning: if reading this book on the back of a catfish statue, the text may vanish at any moment, and you may forget that it ever existed.

From the mind of Toh EnJoe comes Self-Reference ENGINE, a textual machine that combines the rigor of Stanislaw Lem with the imagination of Jorge Luis Borges. Do not operate heavy machinery for one hour after reading.

AND ALSO FEATURING WORK BY HIDEYUKI KIKUCHI

THE FUTURE IS JAPANESE
—EDITED BY HAIKASORU

A web browser that threatens to conquer the world. The longest, loneliest railroad on Earth. A North Korean nuke hitting Tokyo, a hollow asteroid full of automated rice paddies, and a specialist in breaking up "virtual" marriages And yes, giant robots. These thirteen stories from and about the Land of the Rising Sun run the gamut from fantasy to cyberpunk and will leave you knowing that the future is Japanese! Includes Hideyuki Kikuchi's "Mountain People, Ocean People."